NICE JEWISH BOYS

Nice Jewish Boys
By Sarah L. Young

Published by Less Than Three Press LLC

Edited by James Loke Hale
Cover designed by Aisha Akeju

First Edition August 2017
Copyright © 2017 by Sarah L. Young
Printed in the United States of America

Digital ISBN 9781684310661
Print ISBN 9781684310678

To all the beautiful queer Jews out there: you are important and you are loved.

Thank you to my parents and my brother for helping me through this process and through life. Thank you to my editors, Andretta Schellinger and James Loke Hale. So many thanks also to Hadar, Maggie, Marion, and Snevin for keeping me ok. I love you all!

NICE JEWISH BOYS

Sarah L. Young

CHAPTER ONE

Did you see this? asked the text, along with a YouTube link. Avishai smiled as he tapped it open. Noah was always sending him cute animal videos. He stopped smiling, though, when his father's face appeared on the screen, along with the headline "Post-vote conference with Congressman Miller of Georgia." He closed the window and texted Noah, "Not now." Avishai didn't want to focus on his dad now—he'd be home soon enough as it was.

His phone chimed again.

You have to tell him, the text read. Avishai dropped the phone on the counter without responding and went back to cooking. His phone chimed again, and Avishai picked it up once more, but only to delete the two messages, one of which read, *You need to come out to him.* Just then, a third message arrived. *It's not just us, his policies are affecting everyone. I just think that you could change his mind.* Avishai deleted that message too, then clicked on the link again. His pulse rose as he played the video and his father began speaking.

"My religious views," said Congressman Daniel Miller during his post-vote interview, "have nothing to do with the way I voted today."

Avishai muttered, "Bullshit," under his breath as the video continued playing.

"This isn't about tolerance, or acceptance, and my vote was not shaped by my religious beliefs, which have no place in Congress," he continued, leaning into the sea of microphones and reporters. "This is about special protections under the law, which members of the gay community are not entitled to. If one of them is attacked, the attacker will be punished no less, and certainly no more severely than any other criminal. I reiterate, this is not about tolerance of the gay community, and my vote was not influenced by religion, as the media has so brazenly suggested." Avishai scoffed and clicked out of the link. He put down his phone and went back to his dinner preparations. Cooking always calmed him down, and today he definitely needed that.

His dad was trying to play down the whole "religious" thing, especially since Trump had been elected. He had narrowly won re-election, and some pollster had said that being a religious Jew had not necessarily helped. The fact that the first year of this, his third term, was coming to a close, made it an all-out "suck up to the voters" kind of conference.

Like the rest of Congress, his dad was stuck in an endless cycle of re-election, and it seemed like he spent more time sucking up to increasingly anti-Semitic voters than getting work done on Capitol Hill.

His father was still just as Jewish, but it was no longer as highly publicized as his other attributes: widower, single father, a former assistant district attorney with an admirable conviction record, and a popular politician among his constituents. Avishai wished that his religion was *actually* a lesser part of him, in private as well as in public.

If that were the case, then maybe he could be truthful with his father. But he knew it wasn't. His father wasn't as accepting as his press secretary would have the public believe. In fact, he would kick Avishai out if he found out that he was gay — that he was in love. Avishai wanted to share that love with his father, with his classmates, with everyone he knew.

But no one could know, and no one would ever know. His dad's vote yesterday, the one *against* stricter punishment for LGBT hate crimes, had just affirmed that.

No matter whom he told, it would get back to his father. Eventually, of course, it would also get back to a teacher at the Academy, and as much as he disliked his school, he didn't want to get expelled like the last kid to come out there.

No, he texted back to Noah, but before he could even place his phone down, a response appeared, asking why. Avishai sighed as he reiterated the list he told himself every day when the urge struck to reach for Noah's hand at school. *Because it isn't worth getting expelled and sent to straight camp over. The JONAH program is no joke, kids there turn crazy, not straight.* He knew he was being a little harsh with Noah, but geez, how many different ways could he say the same thing before his boyfriend finally got it? He wasn't going to come out.

You're right, came the response, several minutes later. Avishai had gone back to his cooking and the noise of his phone startled him. He stared at the clock before responding, *Let's just forget about this, I'll talk to you after Shabbat. I love you.* He watched the phone, waiting for a response.

Yeah, was all he got back.

Fine. If Noah didn't want to be an adult about this, he didn't have to be.

Avishai deleted all the messages, turned on some music to sing along to, and went back to his cooking. His dad would be home soon, and dinner had to be ready. Things had to go a certain way, and they would. His dad would get home from DC, they'd discuss school and work, and then they'd go to bed. If he could sleep as late as he wanted, there would only be a few hours before Shabbat was over and he could text Noah again. He could make it that long. He could pretend to be straight for that long.

A few minutes passed before he heard his dad's key slip into the door. He took a deep breath, preparing himself for the weekend. "Hey, kiddo," Avishai's dad called as he opened the front door. "How was school?"

"It was good," Avishai responded. "How was work?"

"Fine." And he went upstairs to change.

Like every week, that was all he said after arriving home after a week in DC, but Avishai pretended not to notice, let alone mind as much as he did. He quickly went through his mental checklist to make sure everything was the way it had been last Monday when his father had left. Nothing could be suspicious. He turned up his music to combat the sound of his father lumbering up the stairs, the well-concealed high school footballer showing himself after hiding in a suit all week.

Avishai and his father had never had a particularly strong or loving relationship. They had never been comfortable around each other, and it had only gotten worse since his mom died nearly five years ago. They weren't the sort of people who could sit together silently and simply take pleasure in each other's company.

Their differences had become more apparent as they aged. His dad only wanted to do something with him if it involved a ball getting thrown around. Avishai didn't like playing, watching, or listening to sports. God forbid they do something that Avishai would enjoy, like see a concert, or go to a museum.

Avishai had tried to play sports as a child, but was never particularly talented or interested. As he grew older but not much larger, his mom had taken him off the soccer bench and moved him to the piano bench, which he'd found to be a much more comfortable fit. His mother had taught him, and as they got closer, his father seemed to become more distant. Avishai was reminded of this disconnect, his dad's disinterest in him, daily as his father's trophies were on a shelf proudly displayed in the living room, whereas his own medals and certificates from music competitions were stacked in a box somewhere in the attic.

"Turn off that music, it's almost *Shabbos*," snapped his dad suddenly, startling Avishai. He hadn't even heard him come down the stairs, but according to the clock on the wall, it had been a few minutes since he'd gone upstairs.

"Sorry," he muttered, scurrying to turn the music off as his father headed into the dining room. It was almost sunset—time to light the candles.

"Ready?" asked his father as Avishai rounded the corner into the dining room, where he was already seated at the head of the table.

"Sure." Avishai grabbed the matchbook, candles, and candlesticks, and set them on a small tray on the table, next to where his father sat. His dad lit the candles, symbolizing the beginning of *Shabbos*. Normally the matriarch of the family lights the candles, but after his mom's death, his dad had taken up that responsibility. *"Baruch atah Adonai, eloheinu melech haolam, asher kidshanu b'mitzvotav vitzivanu, lehadlik nair shel shabbat,"* his dad said, reciting the prayer over the *Shabbos* candles.

"Wanna lead *kiddush* or should I?" asked Avishai, already knowing the answer. *Kiddush* was the blessing said over the *Shabbos* wine—or, in their case, grape juice. His dad sort of nodded and waved in Avishai's direction after pouring a himself a glass and handing the bottle to Avishai. "Here," he said, and they stood for the *kiddush*, as was tradition.

Avishai sang the blessing, his voice tired from the day's performance at school, then raised his glass to his father's.

"*L'chaim*, to life," they said together as they clinked glasses. His dad drank the sweet juice, but Avishai put down the glass after having only touched the liquid to his lips. *Gross*, he thought to himself. That stuff tasted like cough syrup, he didn't get how his dad liked it so much.

Avishai looked at his father, waiting for him to deliver the blessing parents give to their children on Friday nights.

"Hang on a sec," his dad told him. He gulped his last mouthful of juice, then sighed and slowly stood up. And, slower yet, he walked to Avishai and placed a large hand on his head.

"*Y'simcha Elohim, k'Ephriam v menashe,*" he began. "*Yivarechecha Adonai yishmarecha, yaer Adonai panave lecha vichunecha, yisa Adonai panave lecha viasem lecha shalom.*" The blessing asked that his son be like other great men of the Bible. Then he kissed the top of Avishai's head gently, but only for a moment.

Avishai followed him to the kitchen so he could take the hand-washing cup, fill it with water, and pour it on his hands over the sink. Then he said the blessing, refilled the cup, and handed it to his father. His father did the same, and they silently returned to the table. Jewish law forbade them from speaking between the blessing for washing hands and the prayer over bread. The silence wasn't much of a difference for Avishai and his father, though.

His father sat and rested his head in his hands. Avishai returned to the kitchen and took the *challot*, the braided bread made specifically for *Shabbos*, still warm from the oven. He put them on a plate and covered them with the special *challah* cover he had made with his mom when he was six.

He started toward the table, humming the song *Eli Eli* to himself. Although he could not speak, there was nothing wrong with humming. The school choir had sung it that day at assembly, and the lyrics played softly through his mind. The English translation was beautiful: "*Lord, my God, I pray that these things never end: the sand and the sea, the rush of the waters, the crash of the heavens, the prayer of man.*"

Avishai knew how the writer, Hannah Senesh, felt. He prayed that his and Noah's love would never end. He quickly turned his thoughts back to dinner, and delivered the bread to the table with a skip in his step. He uncovered the bread in front of his father. When he was little, his mom used to pretend to gasp at the beauty of the bread as he uncovered it, and he would collapse in fits of laughter.

His father barely looked up when he removed the bread's cover.

Avishai finally broke the silence and said the blessing over the *challot* with his hands covering both of the loaves. They were required to have two, something to do with the Israelites in the desert receiving two portions of manna on Friday, one for that day and one for the next. Although he could remember that, he couldn't remember when there had been enough people at their Shabbat dinner to eat two whole loaves.

"*Baruch atah Adonai, Elohainu melech haolam, homotzi lechem min ha'aretz*," he said, delivering the prayer and thanking God for the bread.

"Amen," his father mumbled, cutting an end piece off one of the *challot*. After breaking it in two, he offered half to Avishai.

"What's for dinner, son?" he asked Avishai after he'd finished chewing. "I'm starving."

"Chicken soup, green beans, rice, and bread crumb chicken. I started making it yesterday." Avishai smiled, proud of his work. Okay, so he hadn't started cooking until that afternoon, but he had bought the ingredients and chopped up the vegetables on Thursday. He just wanted his dad to know how hard he'd worked.

"Great. I appreciate it. Need help serving?" he asked, probably more of a reminder to speed it up than a genuine offer to help.

Avishai took the hint. "No, I got it." He hurriedly went back to the kitchen, not dawdling like he had while getting the *challot*. He served the steaming soup in two bowls. His father sniffed appreciatively at the steam coming from his bowl before digging in.

"Careful," Avishai warned. "It's very hot." He stuck his spoon in and blew over the top for a moment before sticking it in his mouth. It was good, but not like his mom used to make it. Nothing ever was.

"So," he said, when the silence had become unbearable, "what happened with that vote?" He fiddled anxiously with his napkin, mentally kicking himself for even bringing it up. Then again, it was all anyone at school was talking about. "Did it pass? Did you want it to?"

Avishai's dad looked at him blankly for a moment as if he had just asked if he was a unicorn, or something equally as ridiculous. "Of course that ludicrous bill didn't pass," he spat. "I can't believe anyone would actually vote for it." Avishai already wanted to change the subject, but he could tell by the look in his dad's eyes that he wasn't going to get the chance. Not by a long shot.

"Do you know what it was about?" his dad asked. Avishai nodded. He had a feeling his dad was going to tell him anyway.

"It's the gays," he said, matter-of-fact.

"They want it considered a hate crime when someone does something to them. It's not a hate crime if it's not a real minority. That's the way I see it, and the last time I checked, the queers aren't considered a minority. They want to be treated special, and be protected from things like getting fired or expelled, but no one ever considers if they've actually done something wrong and deserve it. They want attention for their agenda. They want sympathy to say, 'Look, we face discrimination, give us special treatment, and funding, and anything else we want, and if you don't it's discrimination.' Just because they're different doesn't entitle them to special treatment." He paused and took a sip of water.

Avishai knew what his father was saying were only words, but the tone with which he delivered them cut deep. He wished Noah were there, because he was better at debate and could make his dad see how unfair he was being.

"Get it?" he asked Avishai, who could barely bring himself to nod. He knew that his dad's anger wasn't directed at him, but it might be one day.

"Listen," his dad continued, calming just a little. "I don't understand the gays. I don't think it's right by God, but if they're in America, people can do what they want. Just don't ask me to give them an advantage because of who they sleep with."

19

Avishai nodded again. He cleared the table of the soup dishes on autopilot. Then he put the chicken, green beans, and rice on a tray and put them on the table. He surveyed the spread in front of him but he no longer felt hungry. His stomach was twisting itself into knots.

"Dad, I know you just got home," he began. "But my stomach is really bothering me. I think that I should just get some rest." He turned around and walked back to his room before his father could even respond.

The minute he got to his room, he burst into tears. He'd barely held it in until that point and buried his face deep into a pillow so that his dad wouldn't be able to hear his cries. He tried to calm himself down, but it was no use. Stupid depression—it seemed like he was always in tears. He went to sleep crying, thinking of Noah all the while.

~~*

Avishai slept fitfully that night and woke up with tear stains on his pillow. He got out of bed and went downstairs to clean the dishes from the night before. He thought they would be in the sink, but instead found them clean and neat, all put away. He turned to see his father sitting at the table drinking a mug of coffee.

"Hey," his dad said. "What happened last night? You okay now?"

Avishai looked at his father out of the corner of his eye. Why was he being so nice? Was he feeling guilty about last night? "Uh, yeah. Sure. I just wasn't feeling well. That's all. Why?"

"What do you mean 'why?' I'm your father. I'm sorry I was grumpy last night, it had just been a long week at work. But I care about you, and I know when something's wrong. Now spill it, kid."

Avishai had to keep from rolling his eyes at his father's sudden interest. Nothing good or productive could come from any answer he gave. Silence was not good either, though. Which was the lesser of the two evils? He opted to say nothing.

"Look," said his father after a few minutes of awkward nothingness. "I'm not good at this emotional stuff like your mom was. But you gotta tell me if something is bothering you. Do you miss me during the week? You could move to DC, and we would just come back on the weekends, so you wouldn't have to be alone all the time." He looked hopefully at Avishai.

"Gee, I'd love to, but..." Avishai couldn't think of an excuse, and he couldn't tell him the real reason: that having a house essentially to himself let him and Noah spend as much time together as they wanted. "I, I can't," he stammered. "I'd have to change schools, and leave all my friends from choir and, and... you'd be at work the whole time, anyway."

"Well, okay," his dad said, looking a bit hurt.

"Just keep that offer in mind, in case you ever reconsider. I could get a bigger apartment. You'd make new friends, even find a nice, pretty, Jewish girl?"

Avishai looked up at him nervously. Was he just making conversation, or was he trying to gauge Avishai's reaction to this latest comment about finding a nice Jewish girl? In case it was the latter, he faked a smile. A nice big one. "I'll try my luck with the pretty Jewish girls here." He wasn't sure how convincing he sounded, but his father seemed more than willing to buy it. So that was that.

"C'mon," Avishai's dad said to him after a few moments of saying nothing. "We should start to get ready for synagogue."

~~*

The two of them dressed quickly and walked the few blocks to their synagogue. It was *Rosh Hodesh*, the beginning of the new month, so they would be doing *Hallel*, an extra set of prayers, in addition to the weekly service. The rabbi had announced last week that today was also a Bar Mitzvah, so the service would last extra-long.

Avishai and his dad walked together into the sanctuary. They were early, so most of the people there were relatives of the Bar Mitzvah boy. Out-of-towners always got there on the early side, not knowing how long the service would go and also not wanting to miss anything.

They sat down in their regular spot near the doors. Five minutes in, Avishai was itching to get up. Synagogue was never all that interesting, at least to him, and tonight's extras meant the service would take forever. When the cantor had finished and sat down, the Bar Mitzvah boy got up. He looked around nervously.

Poor kid, Avishai thought. He remembered his own Bar Mitzvah. He'd been so nervous, and he hadn't been well prepared. His father had decided to teach him, but as a district attorney trying to break into the world of politics, he hadn't had free time. Avishai had ended up just listening to recordings of his Haftarah until he had practically memorized it.

When the day had come, his hair wouldn't lie flat, his voice was cracking, and the lack of eating from all the stress caused his pants to be quite loose. The belt did little, and he spent most of the service with a firm grip on his trousers. He'd been just as deer-in-the-headlights as the kid standing before him now.

Regardless of all the things that the poor kids had to go through for this rite of passage, the services were still mind-numbingly boring to all those in attendance.

Avishai surveyed the crowd, from the rabbi, who was sitting on the *bimah*, to the Bar Mitzvah boy's parents, where they sat in the front row, a sort of nervous pride on their faces.

Bored and still a little upset over last night's events, Avishai glanced around at the guests for the Bar Mitzvah. In the crowd of out-of-town family members, he found Noah sitting with a tired-looking man and woman Avishai recognized from late-night Facebook stalking as Noah's parents. *Why is Noah here? And why didn't he tell me he was coming?* Had he meant to before they'd started fighting last night? Was he so mad that he hadn't wanted to tell him?

As quickly as possible, he caught Noah's gaze, then darted his eyes at the door. Noah whispered to his parents and then slid out the door and into the hallway. Avishai turned to his father. "Hey Dad, my stomachache is back from last night. I'm gonna go to the bathroom." He feigned pain, looking pleadingly at his father.

Avishai's dad took one look at him and gave him the go-ahead. He was out the door by the time his father could look back to the Bar Mitzvah boy.

As he stepped out into the hallway, Avishai looked around. When he saw no one, he took off in a dead sprint toward the lobby. He only stopped when he saw an elderly couple slowly entering the corridor. He held the door for them, scanning the lobby for Noah, whom he finally spotted standing by the window, his elbows resting on the sill. Avishai looked around once more, and again saw no one else but Noah. He tapped him on the shoulder, then, when Noah spun to look at him, put his arms around his shoulders and kissed him softly. Too quickly, he pulled away, afraid someone would see.

"Hey, Ooshy," Noah teased. No one could call him that but Noah. The nickname had always sounded silly and childish, but Noah had found a way, for Avishai, at least, to make it sound sexy.

"What are you doing here?" Avishai asked him after a moment.

Noah smiled. "Apparently not kissing my boyfriend," he said, and leaned in for another kiss. Glancing around and finding no one else in sight, Avishai complied. After a moment, Avishai thought he heard footsteps and sprung away from Noah. But there was no one there. Just his imagination.

"Really though," whispered Noah after a moment of silence. "When Dad came home last night and said that a coworker's kid was having his Bar Mitzvah here and that we were going, hell, I wasn't gonna complain!"

Avishai wasn't going to either. "C'mon," he said, smiling broadly, and showed Noah to the vacant youth lounge.

CHAPTER TWO

Avishai fell onto the couch in the youth lounge and they were full-on making out within a few seconds. He didn't care about last night anymore. It reminded him of when they had first started dating, both scared freshmen thrust together for a project. While studying and collecting resources for the project, they had ended up kissing. Even though they'd known there was something inherently wrong, it had also seemed kind of perfect, like they didn't need words to explain what they felt.

After the kiss, they hadn't spoken for a few days. Still, it was all either of them had thought about. How could they not?

They'd avoided each other in the halls, not even making eye contact. They'd each finished their part of the project separately, and had only combined it the morning it was due.

Then one day, Noah had stopped Avishai in the hall. He'd grabbed his arm and dragged him to a secluded, empty corner of the private section of the school's study rooms. The richest kids at RHA had their own rooms, and apparently, this subsection of students included Noah.

"Look," said Noah after he'd locked the door.

"What happened...happened. Maybe it shouldn't have happened, really, but, um..." He'd trailed off, and Avishai had taken his chance.

He'd moved in to kiss Noah. It had been awkward, at first, but got better with time. Noah had pulled him in, and they'd kissed for several moments, neither wanting it to end. Avishai had felt as if all his troubles were melting away. His grief, his concerns from school, the fear that someone would know what he was doing. All… gone.

This had been going on for two years, now. It was a pure, unconstrained sort of love. They missed each other whenever they were apart, and relished each moment together.

They spoke constantly—in person, through FaceTime, texts, and on the phone. They spoke about everything imaginable, from their homework to politics, their home lives to Ancient Rome.

One subject they spoke of often was Avishai's mom. Noah had never met her, but she was such an important part of Avishai's life that he needed to know all about her, like that she had had a brief battle with breast cancer before she had died. That his dad hadn't known how to deal with Avishai when she was gone, so he'd thrown himself into his campaigning. How that made Avishai feel, how everything involved made him feel. Noah had helped Avishai through the grieving process, even though by the time they met, his mother had been dead for two years.

Everything they spoke about suddenly became the most exciting thing in the world. Nothing mattered but their discussions. They were all that existed. It was what got them through long, boring, difficult classes, knowing that during lunch and study hour, that they would be "studying" in Noah's room.

The only thing they never spoke of was what would happen if someone found out. Noah sometimes asked him if he was ready to come out, but he knew it would never be an option. By now they both knew the consequences: they would most likely be kicked out of their homes, expelled, and then turned to the streets with nothing. That obviously couldn't happen, which was why they had told no one.

No one knew about this. If anyone knew, soon everyone would know, and that just couldn't happen. The only way they could stay together was to keep it a secret, for as long as it took.

~~*

Avishai held Noah in his arms and kissed him deeply, as if to apologize for the night before. "I'm sorry," he told Noah after breaking away. "I just get so paranoid when I have to talk to him about anything gay. I'm just so scared that he'll somehow know."

Noah nodded sadly. "You're right. I just feel

like if someone talked to him he might change his mind and then we could be out and—"

Avishai cut him off. "That's not the way it works, and you know it. There are a lot of reasons we can't come out, not just my dad. We just need to deal for now, and you need to be okay with sitting still." Noah nodded again, looking defeated. "Kiss and make up?" Avishai suggested, and Noah smiled broadly as he went in to kiss him again. After another moment, though, Avishai had to pull away. "We have to get back in there— or at least I do—or my dad's gonna think I'm ditching."

"Whatever, goody two shoes," Noah replied with a laugh. Avishai got up to return and Noah blew him a kiss. At least he wasn't mad at him.

He returned to the sanctuary, his lips still buzzing from kissing Noah and his heart still aflutter, just as the Bar Mitzvah boy was starting his sermon. He slipped in beside his father and watched the Bar Mitzvah boy clear his throat. "Shabbat shalom," the Bar Mitzvah boy squeaked.

"Where were you?" demanded his father. He looked more impatient than angry, but he didn't think his dad would be mad about him using the bathroom.

"Sorry, sorry," said Avishai. "My stomach is just still really bothering me." He did his best to look pained, and it must have worked because his dad looked satisfied. They each turned back in their chairs and were silent to each other throughout the rest of the service.

Later on, during the luncheon in honor of the Bar Mitzvah boy, Noah walked up beside Avishai. He was thankful for the distraction that Noah's presence represented. There were so many people milling about, all of them trying to ask Avishai about college plans and school and what he was doing this week and other things that neither he nor they really cared about. He found this whole process draining and wished people would stop pretending to give a damn about him just to get some clout with his father.

"What's up?" Avishai asked.

"A few kids from RHA are sitting together. Wanna go?" asked Noah, broad smile on his face. He had always been more social than Avishai, and had many friends both at school and Jewish camp.

"Uh, sure," Avishai replied, not actually sure of anything. He knew all the RHA kids who would be there and wasn't a friend of any of them. There would be, of course, the guys from the soccer team: Jacob, Noam, Amichai, and Jeremy. Their girlfriends would also be present. The girls' clique was called the matriarchs, as their names were Sarah, Rivka, Rachelle, and Leah. These kids had all gone to the Academy since preschool or kindergarten, and they felt that gave them the right to rule the school. No one was eager to correct them.

As Avishai walked over to the group, he saw the smiling face of someone he'd never met, but she looked oddly familiar. He looked quizzically at Noah, who said, "Avishai, this is my sister, Hadar."

They shared a strong resemblance, Noah and his sister. Noah had never let Avishai come to his house or meet his family, being as paranoid as he was about getting caught, but he had talked to Avishai about his sister constantly. From what Avishai had heard, they were both very alike in personality, and looking at them, he could tell they were siblings; each had curly black hair that was set off by their remarkably pale complexions. They even carried themselves with the same confidence. Avishai had never met her, so that was all he really knew about her. That, and knowing Noah desperately wanted to come out to her even though she would probably end up telling everybody.

"Hey, great to meet you, Hadar!" Avishai said to the thirteen-year-old, extending his hand. She, in turn, grasped it with a smooth, delicate hand. Her eyes moved from him to her brother and back again questioningly.

Avishai thought he saw Noah give a small nod to his little sister before she turned back to Avishai, with a broad grin as she replied, "It's *amazing* to meet you too, Ooshy."

CHAPTER THREE

That night in bed, he shivered. Did Hadar know? If not, why call him the pet name Noah had come up with, the one only he used? If she knew, then how? He had wanted to talk to Noah about this after the luncheon but Noah was hanging out with friends; they didn't get a single minute alone. He had always been so eager to come out, had he risked it and told her? Without even telling him? Avishai chased that thought away. He knew Noah had been frustrated the night before, but he couldn't imagine he would have done anything like that. Could she have gone through his phone messages? That last possibility snapped Avishai out of his thinking. Had *he* remembered to clear the messages from his phone?

He quickly pulled his phone from his pocket to check, suddenly panic-stricken. He unlocked the screen and checked the messages. He'd erased the ones from Noah, thank God. His dad always claimed that a right to privacy was fundamental— after all, he was a Republican—but Avishai wouldn't put it past him to sort through his own son's messages.

Avishai and Noah texted constantly. Nothing was outright inappropriate or incriminating, partially because the two were so decided in wanting to abstain from sex until marriage. In fact, the messages Noah sent him every morning when he woke up and every night when he went to sleep were sweet, and sometimes the highlights of his day. Most of the stuff they texted was pretty chill, though—just conversations that any two friends could have.

Yet, if someone were to see the messages that contained the words "I love you," especially his dad, it wouldn't be good. Avishai and Noah each erased all messages when they finished reading them, but Avishai kept a notebook where he recorded certain messages. That notebook was hidden inside his teddy bear. The bear had been given to him by some great aunt, and in it had been a small music box. The music box had died, and when he had taken it out, it left a perfect hidey-hole for something like a small notebook.

Although Noah liked to text, Avishai preferred to call because that way they had nothing to erase, nothing to hide. That, and it was so much more personal. If someone asked why they were on the phone, they could always say one had called the other for help with homework. The best calls were late at night, when they could almost imagine they were in bed together.

Avishai pulled out the notebook and flipped to his favorite text, the first time Noah had texted him "I love you." Their first anniversary had been a few days before, but they had had a fight and "I love you" was the first thing Noah texted him afterward.

The fight had started on their anniversary, and after having had such a nice day. They had been on the phone all evening, staying up until midnight so they could reach their anniversary together. It was cheesy, but Avishai had wanted to do it. They'd been just breathing into the phone, Avishai trying his hardest to stay awake. He'd known he was in love, but had been too afraid to admit it. It had made things that much more real and the secret that much bigger.

"You still up?" Noah had whispered into the phone. It was hours past when Avishai should have been asleep, but while lying in bed speaking to Noah, sleep was the furthest thing from his mind.

"Yeah," breathed Avishai. He smiled, just thinking of Noah lying there, probably drifting closer and closer to sleep as each moment ticked by. Comforted and encouraged by this thought, he took in a deep breath and gathered all his feelings from the past year he'd spent with Noah.

"Noah, I'm in love with you," he said, with little flourish. Waves of embarrassment immediately washed over him and he felt his face grow hot. He waited anxiously for Noah's reply, and relaxed when he could practically hear Noah smile over the phone.

"Ooshy, I love you, too."

It had felt as if a giant weight had been lifted.

They'd stayed up all night talking, not really planning on going to school in the morning. Avishai had heard when Noah's alarm clock went off, and he'd giggled because school was so far from his mind. They'd only hung up to tell their parents that they were sick and unable to go to school that day. It had been easier for Avishai, as all he needed to do was call his father in DC, and sound sick. The two had spent the day as they had spent the night: together. Around nine o'clock in the morning, Noah took a bus and by nine thirty he was at Avishai's house.

For a long time, all they'd done was lay in each other's arms. For the first time Avishai could remember, he'd been happy just being in someone's company, completely satisfied with the silence of a moment.

Later on they'd finally gotten up, and when they had, they couldn't keep themselves from smiling, so in love they could do nothing else. Avishai had known, however, that they would need to have a real conversation about the night before. They'd done plenty of talking, but none of it about what was to come.

"Do you realize we've been together a year now?" Noah had asked Avishai.

Avishai had laughed. "Yeah. We've lasted longer than some marriages, you know. It's weird to think about, but this, whatever it is, is for the long run. We've stayed together longer than most of the couples at school."

Noah had looked at him, his mouth falling into a frown. "I love you, Ooshy, and you love me. It should just be that simple," he said forlornly.

Avishai'd looked back at him, slightly confused. "What do you mean? It *is* that simple. We're in love, we spend time together, we share secrets. We're just like any regular couple."

"See?" Noah had whined. "Even you don't get it. The fact that you say 'regular,' 'normal!' Like we're somehow not. That even you, supposedly the love of my life, don't even view us, or yourself, for that matter, as normal." Avishai had reached to put his hand on Noah's shoulder, but Noah had brushed him off, clearly irritated. Avishai had understood the frustration, but why did Noah have to be so confrontational about it? They didn't plan to come out anytime soon, so why always fight about it? It only ever made Noah annoyed and Avishai sad.

"It makes me think that you don't ever want people to know about us," Noah had continued, sounding hurt. "About the love that we share, the commitment and trust we've built. We shouldn't have to hide this; love should be celebrated, in all forms! To me, this is real. You are real. Our love is real. It doesn't, or at least shouldn't, need to be validated. Not by society, not by our classmates, not by our parents.

"I just need to tell someone, though," he continued. "Someone needs to know how happy I am, and that it's because of you. Someone needs to know so that I don't have to feel like I'm sneaking around all the time. Someone needs to know so that I can feel, for the first time, that this isn't wrong, that love isn't wrong. I need to tell someone!"

When he was done, Avishai'd had tears in the backs of his eyes. They had stayed silent for a moment. Avishai had opened his mouth to speak, but couldn't find the words. Of course he wanted the same things. He wanted everyone to know. He wanted to tell the world that he was in love, that for the first time since his mom had died, he was truly happy, and nothing could bring him down. Nothing except his father turning against him, which is what he'd be risking by coming out. He couldn't. His father was his only family, regardless of their difficult relationship.

"Noah, of course I want people to know. I know how hard this is for you, and it's just as hard for me. But people can't know. It's simply not an option. You know what would happen. But it's okay, we can do this. We can figure this all out. Our love can stay a secret for a little while more."

He'd looked at Noah for a few moments before he could take no more of his tearful gaze. He'd watched as Noah stood slowly and left. He didn't see or hear from him for three entire days before Noah called him, saying that he was right, that they couldn't let anyone know. And that was the way it had stayed.

CHAPTER FOUR

Avishai had decided not to ask Noah about Hadar over the phone unless Noah brought it up, which he probably wouldn't. On the phone when they spoke, Noah hadn't been at all chatty— almost despondent, actually. Maybe it was because of this. Avishai thought it might be, but was determined that if something was wrong, he would address it straight on, not hide behind a phone. It just so happened that the next chance they got together was on Monday during *Mishna* class.

Avishai hated the class, but Noah was merely indifferent to it. Most classes he loved, and was therefore unwilling to miss even a few moments. They had a system for missing classes, and it worked so that they missed five minutes from *Mishna* on Mondays, five minutes from *Gomorrah* on Wednesdays, and fifteen minutes from Hebrew on Fridays because the teacher was old and it was a ninety-minute class, so he didn't really care. The two of them were in totally different social circles, so in a school as clique-y as the Academy, no one would believe they were friends if they were seen together. Or at least that was what Noah had told him, and who was he to argue?

Teachers so far hadn't picked up on Avishai's system, and Noah didn't mind so long as he got his time with Avishai. Of course Avishai had a plan in place in case any of their teachers started to grow suspicious. They would stop meeting for a while, then resume during *different* classes. The two needed this time alone together.

Avishai started their routine at exactly eleven thirty, same as always. He sneezed a few times—by this point he was good at pretending—and looked around for a tissue. As none of the classrooms at RHA ever had them, he would then ask his teacher if he could go to the bathroom to blow his nose.

At 11:32, Noah would ask to use the bathroom. They would never go there, though. They always went to Noah's private study room, as Avishai now had a key, too.

Avishai would arrive first, followed closely behind by Noah. On this particular Monday, Avishai was nervous for Noah to arrive. He fidgeted with his hands and licked his lips as he planned out what exactly he'd say.

Noah walked in, looking ashamed. Avishai opened his mouth to speak, but Noah cut him off.

"I have a confession to make," he began. "Hadar knows. She saw us go into the youth lounge, and I guess she must have figured that something was going on, because we were holding hands. I'm so sorry, Ooshy." He kept his eyes locked on his trembling hands.

Avishai was mad, but at himself rather than at Noah. He should have been more careful. He should have checked the entire hallway, not just the part across from the youth lounge. How could he have been so stupid? This was more his own fault than Noah's.

After a moment of thought, he asked, "Did she tell your parents?" If she had, it was all over. Everything was.

"No, thank God. She came to me right after we got back. She didn't even ask me, just said, 'I know you're with that kid with the short brown hair. I'm happy if you are, and I won't tell if you don't want me to.' Then she asked what your name was, how long we'd been together, if we were in love, and if anyone knew. Basic stuff like that. I couldn't lie to her. I mean, she's my sister, and I love her, plus she's completely trustworthy. She would *never* tell. She knows what this means to us, what telling someone would mean. I'm so, so sorry, Ooshy. I really didn't mean for this to happen." He looked pleadingly at Avishai.

Avishai knew this was an accident and hoped Noah was telling the truth, but the anxious part of his brain kept telling him that maybe Noah had done this on purpose, as a test, to see how people would respond. Avishai wanted to believe he wouldn't do something so careless. This relationship meant so much to each of them, and despite Noah's insistence that Avishai should come out to his father, Avishai didn't think Noah would jeopardize their secrecy that thoughtlessly. Plus, he looked so guilty, and he wasn't the one who'd linked their hands outside the youth lounge…

At least it seemed like things with Hadar had turned out for the best, for now. What was done was done.

"Hey, Noah, it's fine," he said, trying to convince himself as much as he was trying to convince Noah. "Really. You said she's trustworthy, and I trust your judgment. It'll be okay, I promise. And hey, now you can talk to someone about this. We have to go back to class now, but we can talk about this later. I love you, Noah." He gave Noah a kiss and a hug.

Noah turned to wipe his eyes as he was leaving the room. Avishai wasn't sure how much he believed what he was saying, but seeing Noah so upset told him that this had been an accident. And who knew, maybe it all would be for the best.

"I love you too, Ooshy," Noah whispered softly as he closed the door.

Avishai walked from the entrance of the study room area into the rest of the school, padding slowly down the hallway. Noah was about a minute ahead, maybe already back in class. Over the years they had gotten quite good at this, sneaking around.

Could all this be in jeopardy? he thought to himself on the way back to class. *All of our secrecy for nothing?* He *did* trust Noah's judgment of Hadar's trustworthiness, but then again, who wouldn't say that their own sister was trustworthy? Who really knew if she would tell anyone, even by accident?

They needed to be more careful, and they couldn't let anyone know. Well, they couldn't let anyone *else* know. That couldn't happen. Anger surged through Avishai. It already *had* happened. It wasn't fair, he thought as he entered the classroom. Their love was the only thing he still had in the world that brought him happiness. It wasn't even imaginable that it could, with just one little indiscretion, all disappear.

Their love, their perfect little secret—how long could they keep it up? How long could Hadar resist the urge to run to her parents, or even a friend, and say what she had seen, what she now knew? What would happen then?

At the Rosenbaum Hebrew Academy, they had an hour between when fifth period ended and when the buses arrived to ferry the students home. As there was never a staff member to check in on them, students could technically do whatever they wanted. This was another time when Avishai and Noah liked to meet.

Avishai ran a few minutes late that day. He was distracted all throughout his fifth-period class, chemistry, thinking about Hadar and what might happen. His anger had shifted to her, even though it was his own indiscretion that had caused this. He didn't hear the bell ring, and only got out of his chair when his teacher shook him gently, saying, "Hello, Earth to Avishai, class is over."

When he got to Noah's study room, he slipped his key into the lock, only to realize it was already unlocked. He twisted the knob and pushed on the door. When he opened the door, he found two figures in the room instead of just the one he had been expecting.

Noah and Hadar sat in two of the room's three chairs. Although he hadn't been expecting it, Avishai couldn't say he was surprised by this scene, but he wasn't pleased, either. Slowly, he walked into the room, then sat in the only remaining chair when Noah motioned to it.

"Hey, Avishai!" Hadar said excitedly. "Sorry I sort of ambushed you the other day. I didn't realize how big of a deal this is to you guys. I swear, though, I won't tell a soul. Ever. I promise." She looked apologetic and sincere.

Avishai immediately felt bad that he had ever been angry at her. After all, she was just a little eighth grader who loved her brother. "Hey, no problem," he replied after a moment, trying to appear nonchalant. "If someone knows, I'm glad it's someone we can trust." He had no idea whether or not he could trust her, but it was better to make nice. Fake it 'til you make it, right?

"So, uh…" He looked at Noah, then back to Hadar. "What brings you here?"

Noah smiled broadly as he said, "We're all going to have a conversation about this. You two can get to know each other, and she can ask any five questions she wants about our relationship. Plus, Hadar is in the middle school building this year, but next year she'll be up at the high school with us, so I think it would be good for you guys to get to know each other!"

He looked so pleased with this little arrangement that Avishai felt bad voicing his concern. But he had to ask, "Do we have any veto power? With the questions, I mean. Like, if she asks something really personal or private."

Noah's smile faded slightly, like he hadn't really thought about it, as he said, "Sure, let's say that each of us can veto two questions. We have to answer five questions, though." He looked around at all the faces in the room as he said this.

As no one objected, he said, "Okay, let's start. Hadar, what's your first question?"

She looked thoughtful for a moment before looking at Avishai. "When and how did you and Noah start dating?" She switched her gaze from Avishai to her brother and back again, waiting for an answer.

Noah spoke first. "It was the beginning of freshman year. We were both new to RHA because we had just moved and Avishai had been at public school. We were doing a project together. I was at Ooshy's house, and, I don't know, it just sort of started." He shrugged, as if it wasn't really a big deal. He also neglected to mention the part where, after they'd kissed, they hadn't spoken for days.

"Um... okay," Hadar began. "Have you ever come out to anyone?" She posed it to both Avishai and Noah. She asked the question so simply, like it wasn't even a big deal.

Noah was the first to answer. "Speaking for myself only, no. Avishai?"

"No. I didn't have anyone to tell. There's no one important in my life except Noah and my dad, and I can't tell him." He laughed slightly. "And I think Noah already knows." Smiles around the table.

"Noah, have you ever been to his house or met his dad?" she asked after a moment of hesitation. Then, looking back at Avishai, said "I've never seen you over, or even tagged in things on Facebook. So I'm assuming you're never at our house, but does Noah go to your house?"

"He comes over to my house because I'm alone during the work week while my dad's in DC," Avishai said. "We decided it wouldn't be a good idea to hang out over at your house, though. We can't risk getting caught, especially by our parents. I don't know if Noah told you this, but my mom died a few years back, and my dad and I aren't really that close. Honestly, I don't think I would tell him if I had a girlfriend, either." Noah reached for Avishai's hand under the table, and Hadar looked apologetic. Most people appeared that way when they heard about his mom, and it got old after a while.

"I'm so sorry, Avishai, I had no idea about your mom. Do you mind me asking, what happened? Was she sick? Was she in an accident?"

"Stage four breast cancer. She only lived for six weeks after the diagnosis. That was four years ago." He ran through his explanation quickly, answering the questions he didn't want people to ask before they even had the chance. They were all quiet for a moment.

"Why don't we continue?" Avishai suggested after the silence had grown uncomfortable. The siblings nodded, and the questions resumed.

"Do you guys go to gay clubs?" she asked, obviously excited by the prospect. Noah and Avishai laughed.

"Not really my scene," Avishai answered. "Nothing involving dancing, strobe lights, or alcohol really interests me."

"Fair enough. Is this my fifth question?" Hadar asked. Seeing them nod, she went on to deliver her final question. "This is a little more personal, but…" She leaned forward intently. "Have the two of you ever had sex? With each other or anyone else?"

Avishai answered quickly. "No. We are in love, and it would be plenty special, but we've…"

He trailed off.

Noah, answering his sister's questioning glance, said finally, "We've decided to wait until we get married."

CHAPTER FIVE

There was a momentary stunned silence in the room. Avishai looked at Noah cautiously and then back to his sister.

Hadar broke into a huge grin.

"We'll wait until we're older, of course," Noah started, smiling widely. "To get married, that is. We'll be on our own, anyway, because we will have moved out, so we won't need to depend on Mom and Dad for financial or parental support. When we're older, maybe we'll have kids. It'll be amazing." His hand moved to Avishai's back. Avishai tried to smile back supportively. After all, this was what he wanted. This was the life he had planned with Noah.

Although he didn't know exactly why, Avishai began to cry. His cheeks got hot with embarrassment and frustration as the tears welled in his eyes. Now that someone finally knew, someone who was so amazing and supportive, he should have been squealing with joy. This—coming out and being supported—had always been the end goal, right? And what Noah wanted? What their relationship needed.

Noah quickly wrapped his arms tightly around Avishai. "Baby, what's the matter?" he breathed into Avishai's embrace.

"I'll never know what my mom would have done," he answered finally, chest heaving with each labored breath, voice still shaky. "Would she have loved me still? Talked Dad out of kicking me out? Would she hate me? Would she have protected us, danced at our wedding? I'll never know these things, because she never knew about me."

"Ooshy, look. I don't know. You don't know, and we will never be able to find out what she would have done, but a part of her is in you. You are who you are because of who she was, so we can only assume that she would love you no matter what. Don't trouble yourself with what-ifs. Her memory shouldn't be reduced to that."

Noah's words were so instantly comforting that Avishai dried his tears. Giving Noah one final squeeze, he turned back to Hadar. He didn't feel all the way better, but they were there for a reason, and that reason was to get to know one another. So, he put on a happy face and continued the conversation.

"Sorry about that," he mumbled, grabbing a tissue. "Well, you asked your five questions, but do you have anything else you want to know? I mean, I don't really care if Noah doesn't."

"Of course not!" Noah said with a smile. "The whole point of this was to get you two comfortable around each other. I thought this would be more like pulling teeth!"

They all chuckled and went on asking and answering questions, losing track of time. After a while, Avishai glanced up at the clock and, realizing the lateness of the hour, suggested they wrap up. They walked through the now-dark and empty hallways and corridors, Avishai and Noah holding hands all the while.

~~*

Avishai returned home from school the Friday after that later than usual, almost two hours after school had ended. Since Monday, he had taken to spending time after school with Hadar and Noah, usually in one of their study rooms.

He'd cooked that night's dinner earlier in the week, so it shouldn't have been a problem that he came home so late. And it wouldn't have been, had his dad not come home early.

Avishai got anxious as he neared the house, seeing his dad's car in the driveway. Noah dropped him off at the end of the driveway and Avishai's dread grew as he walked into the house and saw that his dad's shoes were on the mat by the door. Avishai hurried to put the prefood in the oven to warm so as not to keep his dad waiting. When it was in, he went upstairs to his bedroom to change and bid his weekly "Welcome home, how was work?" to his father.

When he got to his room, however, his father

was waiting inside, sitting on his bed. Next to him was Avishai's stuffed bear, a worn notebook in his lap.

"Avishai, could you, uh, come in here, please?" his dad asked quietly, almost timidly, in a voice and fashion very unlike his own. Definitely not his usual loud self.

Heart thumping, Avishai walked in silently, staring directly at the floor in front of his feet.

"So, uhh," his dad began, "is this, a—a phase, or something? Or maybe a one-time deal with this Noah kid?" he asked hopefully, gesturing to the notebook and avoiding eye contact when Avishai finally lifted his gaze.

"Dad, I can explain, I mean, it, it's just... Noah, I mean, um… the notebook, it's just..."

"Look!" his dad said, putting up a hand. "I don't want excuses! Just tell me, have you been lying to me? Are you queer?"

Hot tears welled up in Avishai's eyes and blurred his vision. Not the large tears that are big and loose, which force themselves out and come with hiccups, but the small kind that stung the back of his throat as he tried to choke them down. The only reason he was trying to hold them back was because he was frustrated and tired, and he didn't want his father to see him cry. Some of the tears traitorously slid down his cheeks and he turned away to wipe them from his hot face. He went to look his father in the eyes, but was unable.

His thoughts raced, thinking of possible

excuses. Anything was better than the truth, right? His mind, usually so good at last-minute bailouts, came up blank. He knew he would have to answer sometime, and his father would not drop the subject until he'd either confirmed or denied the accusation. Avishai didn't suppose there was any way of denying it, if his dad had read the notebook. He decided to be honest.

"Dad, I'm in love with him," he said, tears now streaming freely down his cheeks.

His dad remained stoic and expressionless, but Avishai thought he saw him clench his jaw.

"His name is Noah Benowitz," he said quickly. "He goes to my school, he gets good grades, speaks Spanish, plays French horn, and he loves me too. He cares about me. Sometimes I feel like that's more than I can say for you." Avishai looked away so as not to see the hurt he knew would be on his father's face.

"God damn it, Avishai," his dad began, his voice a mix between betrayal, disgust, and exasperation. "I do care about you. Of course I do." He shrank back down with each word, apparently remembering that he was a father, and not a bully. "And I do love you." He cautiously patted Avishai on the shoulder. "I just don't show it always like your mom did. I don't know how—it's not my style. I wish I could ask her what to do about this…I just have no idea. I really just need to think about this," he said as he slowly picked himself up and left the room.

Avishai watched him leave and felt the tears start to dry on his cheeks, leaving sticky tracks. He picked up his newly public notebook and, with a frustrated sigh, heaved it at the ground. He couldn't believe this. They had been so careful—they had deleted their texts, they were almost never seen together in any context, and they'd tried their hardest to keep this a secret. Why was this happening? They had done everything right, and yet here they were. He laid down on his bed, realizing that his head was throbbing and his eyes were stinging. He closed them to ease the pain and before he knew it, he was asleep.

He woke up with a start when his father opened the door and shuffled into his room. Avishai blinked to clear his vision and listened as he heard his father say, "Look, I don't like that you're into guys. The way I read it, the Bible says no, and don't think for a second that I support it, but you're my kid. I can't turn my back on you, you've got nowhere else to go." He seemed almost disappointed in this, like he was stuck with a defect.

He turned away from Avishai and quietly said, "Don't let this get out, though, not yet. The press is going to have a field day, so let's not make it public yet. We should—I mean, you and my office, should decide on what you're going to say. It's best if the tabloids don't find out about it themselves, you know, might cause trouble, rumors, gossip. Less fuss, less upset voters, all that rot." He started pacing, speaking more to himself than to Avishai, who was anxiously wringing his hand and knowing that there was no way this was going to end well.

"You're gonna have to prepare a statement, maybe deliver it on local news, maybe just send it out to the respectable newspapers. We don't want any of those *shmata* gossip magazines to get it first. Talk to this Noah kid, see if you can get permission to say his name, say that you're in love with him, make a nice little story out if it. That way I get the liberal vote in the election next year. Oh, they are gonna eat it up, and the righties aren't gonna care so long as I remind them that I don't condone it, but that I still love my kid, family values, blah blah blah."

He was apparently done spouting exploitative campaign strategies for the moment, or at least was taking a breath, so Avishai thought it as good a time as any to interject. "I'm sorry," he interrupted, his voice betraying his frustration and confusion. "But when the hell exactly did you decide what was best for me, in personal matters, in my own life, which I obviously didn't want you involved in?" He couldn't believe his father would use him as a political pawn. In all of the paranoid scenarios Avishai had imagined, nothing like this had ever happened.

"Now wait a minute!" his dad shouted. "I am —
"

"I mean, this is not your life, not your business.

If I wanted it to be, I would have told you. If I thought you could handle it, I would have told you. Obviously you can't, but maybe it's just 'not your style' or whatever BS answer you gave for not caring about me." By now Avishai wanted nothing more than to hurt and insult his father as deeply as possible. It was cruel and childish and petty, but it felt good.

"You have gone far enough!" his dad screamed. "I do all that I do out of love for you. I came home this weekend early, for you, and I try to at least once a month. I've gone to every parent-teacher conference at your school, for you, and that is more than most parents can say for their children. I pay for a high-class education for your ungrateful ass because I love you and care about your future. I'm not throwing you out right now because I love you, and because even though I don't agree with your lifestyle, I absolutely can't stand parents who abandon their kids. It means that they've given up on the hope that their children can lead healthy productive lives. I find it disgusting and just plain sad. So that's how you know that I love you, or at least you *should* know, but you don't seem to notice."

By this point, his dad was also beginning to tear up, something that rarely, if ever, happened. Especially in Avishai's presence. Each of them took a moment to process the conversation. His dad was the first to speak, and he did so quietly and only after obvious thought and consideration.

"Fine, if you don't want to do anything public, you don't have to, but so help me, if a word of this gets out to the press, or to the Academy..." Avishai gave him a look. He sighed. "At this point, who knows?"

"Noah's sister," Avishai replied. His father stared at him expectantly, and Avishai raised his eyebrows.

"Only one person?" his dad asked. He sighed in relief as Avishai nodded, and rubbed his forehead. "The more people who know a secret, the harder it is to keep under wraps. How old is she?"

"Thirteen, I think. Why?"

"What assurance do you have that she won't tell, that is if she hasn't already told?"

"Well," Avishai began. "We don't really have any assurance. She's smart, loves her brother, approves of me, and she found out this week, so I don't think she could have told anyone yet. She knows better than that. She understands the consequences. She's a good kid." He took a deep breath. "We can trust her."

CHAPTER SIX

After his dad had had his fill of conversation on the topic of Avishai's newly revealed sexuality, they separated for the last hour left before Shabbat started, probably so his dad could go stew in his room. Avishai went right for his phone.

"Noah," he cried the second Noah picked up. "He knows. Dad knows!"

"He—what? Why do you think he knows?"

Avishai felt his pulse quicken as it hit him all over again. His father knew. Everything he'd been afraid of—it was all coming true. "Why do I think he knows? Because he found my notebook. The one I write your texts in. He found it when he came home from DC today, and he ambushed me the second I walked in. Now he wants me to fit into his congressman to world dictator master plan. He's planning this stupid joint press conference about it."

Noah sucked in a breath. "What do you mean?"

"He literally wants me to come out. Publicly. So he can tell the press he still loves me but won't change his political views. He's gonna give a statement and then I give one. But he—" He swallowed. "He wants you to come out with me.

He's so *horrible*, he just…"

"Do it," Noah interrupted softly. "Do what he says. Come out and take me with you. I can't do it without you, and I can't do this for much longer. This it isn't living. I hate this. We sneak around, afraid. We shouldn't be. We need to do this."

"But what about your parents, though?" Avishai asked, scared for Noah. "Won't they disown you? I can't let that happen, and especially not if I'm going to be the one who's responsible. You can't, I won't let you."

"Don't you see?" Noah argued back. "This is a great thing, an opportunity. It could be a blessing in disguise, just like when Hadar found out. If your dad, the conservative Republican Congressman Miller of the seventh district of Georgia, and a religious Orthodox Jew to boot, doesn't kick out his gay kid, then chances are my parents won't either. Maybe that's why he's making you do this, so he can publicly denounce parents kicking out or disowning their gay kids. My parents can be convinced, maybe even by your dad. This will all work out," he promised. It was only minutes before Shabbat began, so they said their goodbyes, fear and dread growing within Avishai. He didn't know how Noah could be so confident in himself and in his parents.

He still didn't know over a week later, when he reached for his phone at 3:37 in the morning of the day of his press conference to see it was Noah calling. He picked up and managed a soft, "Hello."

Was Noah nervous as well? Was he calling to tell Avishai not to do this, or at least calling to tell him not to pull him into this? Avishai's heart raced with all the possibilities.

"I'm outside your house," Noah stated. His voice sounded hoarse, like he'd been yelling or crying. Maybe both.

Wordlessly, Avishai raced out of his room and down the stairs. He turned off the security system and opened the front door to see Noah standing on the front steps, holding a backpack stuffed to the point of overflowing. In the driveway sat his car. He looked scared and shaken, and his eyes were red and puffy.

"Can I, can I..." Noah tried to begin, but Avishai simply pulled him in from the chilly night and, once inside, wrapped his arms around Noah protectively.

"Of course," he answered. He wasn't sure of the details, but he knew for sure that right now, Noah needed a place to stay.

~~*

Noah slowly began to relax once he was inside. Avishai whisked him in, wrapped a blanket around him, and sat him down on a couch. He set a kettle on the stove to make tea, and then joined Noah in the other room.

"Do you want to talk about it?" he asked finally. He didn't want to be too pushy. Noah was still shaking and looked so scared and desperate.

His voice was unsteady when he began to speak. "Hadar thought I should tell them before tomorrow," he began softly, tears dripping down his cheeks. "So at eleven or so, when they were getting ready for bed, I took them aside, told them what was going on. I talked for a few minutes, and… and they didn't say anything.

"I told them about you, and your dad, and what's going to happen tomorrow. They—they just looked at me, and my mom started crying. And then my dad started yelling. They said I was wrong, that what I was doing, what I was—am— is disgusting. They told me that they were going to send me to JONAH. They told me I could never see you again!" And with that, his voice broke again, and he couldn't contain his sobs.

"T-they were going to take me away from RHA. They said that if I don't change, then I'm not their son. They told me I had turned my back on my religion, forgotten my faith, and that if I don't agree to JONAH, I can't live under their roof anymore. And my mom—she just kept crying, and my dad just kept yelling, so I packed a bag and I got in the car. I didn't know where else to go, no one else knows, and I can't take the chance that they'll understand. I'm sorry, I just couldn't..." He trailed off.

"You're sorry?" Avishai exclaimed, shocked. "You've done nothing wrong! It's been me doing this all along. I'm the one who wasn't careful, which is the reason Dad knows. My announcement tomorrow, I didn't have to include you. I shouldn't have. I shouldn't have dragged you into this. This is my fault. Can you ever forgive me?" Avishai pleaded.

The two held each other for several moments, Noah sobbing into Avishai shoulder. Avishai was trying to remain calm for Noah's sake, but he could feel the tears welling in his eyes. This was, after all, his fault. Neither of them wanted to let go of the other, and in the exhaustion and somber mood of the moment, they fell asleep, holding each other on the couch. They slept until eight o'clock, only waking when his dad called to make sure Avishai knew what to do about the announcement.

~~*

"What are we gonna do?" Avishai asked Noah forlornly. The response wasn't comforting, but it was just what Avishai would have expected.

"You go down to your dad's press secretary's office. You'll sit in a room full of reporters. He'll read his statement, and I'll sit next to you while that's happening. He'll say that he loves you and won't try to change you, but that he does not support this, and he will not change his voting and political policies. Just do what your dad and his press secretary told you, and everything will be fine. The next day we'll go to school and deal with the rest of that. There's nothing else we can do."

~~*

Avishai's heart was pounding in his ears as he heard his dad read aloud:

"Good morning. As the representative in Washington for the Seventh District of Georgia, and as a part of this community, I feel the need to be open with you. Recently, my son Avishai came out to me as gay. As his father I of course love him, and although I don't support homosexuality, I still support my son, as any parent should. His partner, however, has been kicked out of his home because of his lifestyle choice, and so he will be living with us for the time being.

"I want this to be a message for all parents of gay, lesbian, bisexual, and transgender teens: You don't have to agree with your children's lifestyles, but you are a parent nonetheless and must act as one, even and especially when it gets difficult.

"I would like to take this time to introduce my son and his boyfriend, and as members of the seventh district family, I ask that you please respect and continue to support them. That's what families do. This is my son, Avishai." Avishai stood and smiled weekly at the press. He heard the click of camera shutters felt a wave of uneasiness, so he soon sat down. "This is Noah, his boyfriend," his dad said, gesturing again to the table. Noah seemed, more confident—he waved at the crowd, nodded, and smiled as they snapped his picture.

"I hate to cut this short," his father began. *Uh-oh,* he thought. His dad was supposed to stay and answer questions with them. "But I've got to get back to DC for a vote. I leave you in the very capable hands of my press team and these two young men." He motioned again at the two of them. "Any questions for me specifically can be sent to my office and I'll answer them as soon as possible." And with that he left the room, followed by only one or two reporters. The rest stayed in the room, quietly waiting.

Claudia, his dad's press secretary, walked in front of the table where Avishai and Noah sat and announced cheerfully, "We'll now be taking a few questions from reporters. Keep in mind, any insulting or offensive terms are grounds for immediate dismissal from this conference." Then she took a seat at the edge of the table, still in full view of the press and with her own microphone in hand. God, the fact that this was newsworthy made him feel sick—he was just a kid with a boyfriend, why did anyone care? He glanced at the reporters with their eager faces and took a deep breath.

The first question came from a newspaper whose name Avishai didn't recognize. A short, balding man stood and said, "Hi, Joey Smith, from the *Clarkson Tribune.* Does this change your

father's mind politically on any of his stances?"
Avishai had been coached on how to answer
questions by Claudia, and this was one he knew
he'd get and had been expecting and prepared for.

"As he said earlier, no. My father would like to
make it very clear that he still represents the same
beliefs and priorities that he always has, which is
the reason he has been elected three times in the
past to serve as a congressman in this wonderful
district of the great state of Georgia. When the
people elected him as a representative, they chose
him because they agreed with his politics and how
they wanted him to represent them in
Washington. He feels that it would be unfair to
not abide by this, and is also adamant that his
ideals have not changed. This has not and will not
change anything. Next question?"

CHAPTER SEVEN

The press conference lasted only a short while, but for Avishai, it seemed to last an eternity. When they got back to his house, the high stress of the situation and the exhaustion and the sleeplessness of the night before led to a near collapse as soon as the two of them walked in the front door.

Avishai breathed a sigh of relief, but knew that this journey was far from over. Still, the day had gone well and he was tired beyond belief. He still didn't get why all of this was newsworthy, but he had learned to stop questioning his father about press image by now. He laid down on the couch for a nap while Noah looked up people's initial reactions to their press conference. Avishai couldn't bring himself to care, he was so emotionally and physically exhausted. He slept fitfully and woke up around five with a crick in his neck and his stomach aching from how hungry he was. He smiled, though, when he saw that he and Noah had received a group text from Hadar saying *Great job, I'm proud of you two!*

He rolled over and saw Noah curled up on the armchair next to the couch, responding to Hadar's text. "What do you want to do about dinner,

Noni?" Avishai asked.

"Do you want to stay here or should I call for take-out?"

Avishai shook his head. "I want to cook." It was sort of a stress reliever. It made him happy and relaxed, and he'd gotten quite good over the years.

He had access to all of his mom's recipes, and using them made him feel just a little closer to her. In the beginning it had been a way to ease his pain, a coping mechanism. Now it was just a fun hobby, with an enjoyable and yummy byproduct.

"Do you want to watch?" he asked after a moment. He knew Noah couldn't boil water, but he'd always told him how much he liked watching him cook.

"Of course, Ooshy," he said with a wry smile.

Avishai prepared the meal, glancing up every now and then at Noah, who was seated at the kitchen island. He first had to sauté the onions, the beginning to almost every recipe his mom had taught him. In a separate pot, he started boiling the rice, then added peppers, tomatoes, and finally black beans to the pan with the simmering onions. He added spices and threw in herbs, and it smelled divine.

He looked over at Noah as he stirred, to see if he was watching. He was, and so Avishai made his motions more exaggerated and dramatic, even at one point sprinkling in salt like that goofy meme. As the rice was boiling and the beans and onions and peppers were simmering in the pan, he turned to Noah and said, "*Moros y Christianos*."

"*Moros y Christianos*?" Noah asked Avishai.

"Yeah," responded Avishai, a hint of a smile playing at the corners of his lips. He loved the way Noah pronounced Spanish. "Yup, I made comfort food. The name is kind of racist, it refers to the beans as the Moors and the white rice as the Christians, but it's still delicious. I thought we could each use some stress eating after today… and I don't even know what's going to happen tomorrow. I can't bring myself to turn on the news. Do you think they're covering it?"

Noah nodded. The big news junkie he was, he had probably read every article about them. Although he feared he knew the answer, he asked, "Is this considered big and newsworthy? I just, I feel like it's not important. There are wars going on, and murderers going on killing sprees, and natural disasters, and lawsuits, and—and—does this matter? I mean, there was a room full of reporters and journalists in that one little press conference. Why does any of this matter? There's so much going on that's more important. Why should it matter that the son of a congressman from who-knows-where in Georgia is queer? It just—it doesn't make any sense to me."

"Ooshy," Noah said gently as he started to set the table and put the rice and beans together in a bowl. "They're just letting the public know now, in December, so that none of the girls our age get their hearts broken in May when they find out that you're uninterested and otherwise unavailable for prom." Avishai couldn't help but laugh at this.

"What can I say?" Noah continued. "I'm dating a celebrity. Pretty soon you're going to get invited to speak at commencement ceremonies, get interviewed by all the fluffy morning talk shows. I mean, within a few weeks, you're going to have teen magazines all over the country begging for the inside scoop on your love life." Soon Avishai was laughing warmly, the tenseness of the morning gone. After a moment, though, he lost his laugh as he thought back to the press conference.

Noah continued, "Soon you'll have a book deal and speaking tours, and you'll be rich and famous, and I'll be your gorgeous trophy husband you tote around just to look pretty." They were both laughing at all of this. That was one of the greatest things that Avishai loved about Noah—he could make anyone laugh and ease any situation with humor. He couldn't believe how heartless Noah's parents must have been to have thrown him out. Avishai had only known him for around two years, but he could never imagine his life without Noah in it.

His parents, who'd brought him into this world, who'd given him life… if they couldn't love and accept—or at least tolerate him enough to not kick him out of their house after seventeen years—then what hope was there for any child? It was truly heart-wrenching. Avishai knew that it would sink in soon for Noah, and he wasn't sure if he was going to be enough family for him to turn to when it did.

~~*

Around six o'clock, the table was set and the food was set out. They sat down to eat just as the sun was setting. Worried Noah wouldn't like his food, Avishai moved his own around on his plate, waiting for Noah to take a bite. After he did, and then hungrily took another and another, Avishai smiled with relief and began to eat his own meal.

"This is incredible," Noah told him after a moment. Avishai smiled and laughed privately before responding with, "Thank you." Cooking was his passion, and he loved getting to share that with the people he cared about. After a moment, though, Avishai's mind retreated to its world of anxieties.

"Noni," Avishai said quietly. "What are we going to do about *shul*? I mean, it could be, or at least it has the very real potential to be, exponentially worse than what school is going to be like. I mean, at school at least there might be at least some people who are okay with this. They're young, we're all Gen Z, aren't we supposed to be more highly evolved, more enlightened, or something? At *shul*, it's going to be all disapproving old people who give dirty looks and tell me that I'm a sinner. I don't think I'm ready for that."

Avishai got very silent as he realized that he'd just summarized Noah's parents and their reactions to Noah's news the night before. "Noni, I'm so sorry about all of this," he blurted, and immediately regretted having opened his mouth in the first place.

"No, you're right," said Noah, stone-faced. "We need to talk about this—our religion, what to do about the people at *shul*. You're right. It is going to be hard. Because of my parents," he added sullenly, "I don't think that I should go to my *shul* anymore. I don't know about you, but your dad will probably make a decision regarding you guys going, and I'll abide by that, I guess."

Avishai frowned. They had so many problems they still needed to fix.

"Well, my *shul* is the more liberal of the two, I guess," Avishai threw in. "And I think that there's a lesbian couple who go there, Lisa and Maria, I think. They only joined a couple months ago, but so far it seems to be going okay. People sit with them and talk with them, and I think there are some people, especially the rabbi, who are okay with them." He thought for a minute. "How about we take this week off from *shul?* Maybe Dad should go alone, and from there I guess we can see how things go. If no one says anything to him, then we'll probably be fine. If people yell at him, or tell him to leave..."

"Got it. We use your dad as a litmus test. If

people are the same to him, chances are that they'll be the same to us. Plus, we'll have all of the RHA kids who go there, and I'm pretty close with Jeremy and Noam. They could probably back me up... What do we do if school doesn't go well, Ooshy?" he asked, the look on his face growing more and more concerned. "I assumed that my parents would stand by my side, but look how well that turned out. I have you, and for the time being, I can stay here. But I don't have a family — not my own, anyway. I don't have a real home anymore. What happens if the teachers aren't okay with our relationship, or the students aren't, or both? What if the administration decides that there is some old rule that they can dig up and use to get rid of us? It wouldn't be the first time they pulled something."

Avishai could see that Noah was getting quite worked up, and for a good reason. The last kid at RHA to come out had done so in the nineties, and he'd gotten kicked out of school *and* his house. He'd had no one to turn to and had hung himself a week later on the school's playground. Avishai had dug up old school newspaper articles on the incident, and none of them had mentioned why he had been expelled. The only reason he knew the real story was from school lore. Every time he felt suicidal, he thought back to that poor kid, and wondered what the school would make up about him to fill in the blanks of the story.

It went without saying that RHA didn't have a

great track record when it came to LGBT issues. On the first day of each freshman seminar, they had a representative from JONAH—Jews Offering New Alternatives to Homosexuality— come to speak for the class. He always mentioned that they offered services that were able to straighten out even the most crooked Jew, or some such bullshit quip.

Students who were suspected of being gay by a faculty member or any other student, or their "concerned" parents, for that matter, were to be referred to the school psychologist, who would in turn send them to JONAH.

Avishai and Noah each finished their dinner in silence, Avishai mulling through the new possibilities as they sprang into his mind. There was such a taboo in their community, in their school especially, that he wasn't sure exactly what to do, and certainly wasn't sure of what to prepare for in terms of the next day. They would have to be surprised, and hope to avoid JONAH.

They were more than a decade into the twenty-first century, but this deep in the South, especially in the Jewish community, and most importantly in a high school...so little had changed. It seemed like all the progress the rest of the country and world was making was null and void here. Their community was standing still.

In terms of their reception back at school the next day, there were so many variables, so many what-ifs that could not all be accounted for, and ones Avishai knew they simply could not fathom. But he knew one thing for sure: the school would not welcome them both back with open arms, nor would the student body.

~~*

As the night went on and Avishai and Noah grew more exhausted, the two of them decided that maybe another night spent sleeping on the couch was not the greatest idea ever. There was bound to be tossing and turning, so why not be more comfortable and try to sleep in a bed?

True to their belief of abstinence, Avishai set up the bed in the house's guest bedroom for Noah. They had, admittedly, slept quite comfortably in each other's embrace, but that had probably just been due to the lateness of the hour and the newly discovered comfort they had found last night in a loved one's arms.

After making the bed, Avishai kissed Noah good night and held him for a moment. "What are we going to do tomorrow, Noni?"

"Well, Ooshy, first we take a deep breath. We walk into school like nothing is different. Nothing really is different, when you think about it. We've always been gay, and on top of that, they've always been homophobes."

Avishai couldn't help but crack a small smile.

"We'll walk in the front door," Noah continued. "We'll put our backpacks in our lockers and go to class, same as always. The only thing that's different now is that people know. We're the same people and they're the same people. They might be assholes, so just try to keep a level head, okay?"

Avishai nodded, knowing that Noah was right. He had to just stay calm. They couldn't change how people would react; they just had to deal with it as best they could.

Noah gave Avishai one last hug and kiss. "I love you, Ooshy!" he sang as he walked down the hall to his room.

"I love you, too, Noni!"

As he lay awake in bed that night, Avishai thought of what could happen, the things he didn't even dare to mention because he feared them so greatly. He was quite fortunate, though, considering. He'd found Noah, and they'd managed to stay together, creating a happiness that had lasted for two entire years. He knew few of their classmates at RHA were as lucky as the two of them.

~~*

Avishai was, in every possible meaning of the term, thoroughly exhausted, but sleep did not come easily that night. He attempted to will himself to sleep, tried relaxation and yoga, and finally pulled out his big book of Jewish fairy tales to make himself sleepy, but nothing worked. He simply had too much on his mind, and it was all just too much to handle. His whole body ached from fatigue and he felt like he wanted to crawl out of his own skin. He wiggled his foot to try to release excess energy, but it didn't do anything to help, just made him more anxious.

Curled up on his bed, he began to cry. Not the silent kind of tears that burned his eyes and his throat, like when his dad had found out about Noah, but the kind that left him with hiccups and a headache and a horrible misty feeling. He was engulfed in a large fuzzy comforter, but he felt far from comforted. He felt lost, but there was nothing to do.

He wanted to call for Noah, to go to his room, to talk with him, to make himself feel better. He wanted it to end, but didn't even know what "all of it" was. He knew that he couldn't kill himself. That that just wasn't—couldn't be—an option. That was what so many people were doing, because things were all just so bad for them. Sometimes he felt like that, too, he admitted to himself, though he never would have said anything out loud.

He didn't know why he felt like this sometimes, and especially now. His father was coming around, and it genuinely seemed like he wanted to help.

His therapist had nonchalantly suggested he had depression. He had said it was mostly grief from Avishai's mother's death and that it would go away with time. It had, so Avishai had stopped seeing him. Only a few months later it had seemed to come back, but Avishai hadn't told his father; he wanted to deal with it himself.

He had thought, once, about what would happen if he did kill himself. What would happen to Noah? His dad? Would the teachers and the students at RHA feel a loss? He wondered this sometimes. He also wondered what he would say if he were to leave a note.

What would it say? Probably that he didn't know what he was doing or why he was doing it. Well, that sort of made what he was thinking silly. Why would you end your life without knowing the reason that you were doing it? Before, it had felt like the weight of everything he'd been hiding had been crushing him. Now all of that was gone, but he still couldn't breathe any easier.

And then there was Noah. Thinking of him had always pulled Avishai back from all of the dark places in his mind. Noah somehow made all of this seem so worthwhile, and then he always hated himself for thinking that way, like Noah didn't make things better. Of course he did. How could he leave Noah behind? He could never do that to him. It just wasn't fair.

After he'd cried out all of his bitter, self-pitying tears, Avishai finally fell asleep. He fell into the kind of deep sleep that you never want to wake up from, but the kind that you have to, because you know that your life isn't over yet. You have to get up because there is more to do, more to learn, more people to love, and more friends to make. Avishai knew he had to get up.

CHAPTER EIGHT

Avishai awoke with a start when his alarm sounded at six the next morning. He'd slept fitfully, waking often. He turned off the alarm and started down the hall to the guest room.

When Avishai walked in the room, he found Noah still asleep, unmoved by the sound of his footsteps. He sat on the edge of the bed and looked at Noah under the mass of blankets. He noticed that there were wet splotches from tears on the pillow. Noah hadn't let himself get so emotional in front of Avishai, but he was definitely hurting, reeling from the loss of his family and home. It nearly broke Avishai's heart to see Noah like that—crumpled in a heap with tears in his eyes.

He decided to wake him with a kiss. He touched his lips softly to Noah's, and Noah stirred, opening his eyes. He saw Avishai and a smile spread across his face. His eyes were now gleaming, not teary. Whatever sadness Noah had dreamt of had left his mind for now.

"Well," he said. "I could most definitely get used to waking up like every morning." He sat up and returned the kiss. "What time is it?" he asked after they broke apart.

Avishai looked down at his watch. "Just after six. We should probably get going around seven if we want to get there on time."

Noah tried to maintain conversation while he was getting ready for school, but Avishai got ready quietly, dreading the day to come. He thought about it all, how there were so many people at school to face. The students, the teachers, the administration... If he knew one thing, it was that they would all have seen the news and would no doubt have an opinion to voice.

~~*

They hurriedly finished preparations for school, ate a breakfast of cereal and juice, and were in the car by seven fifteen. Classes started at seven forty-five, and it wouldn't be good to arrive late. Avishai sort of felt like this was a second first impression. Not a second impression. That was somehow different from what this was: a reevaluation, a reexamination of what had grown to be familiar.

They walked in the door of the Rosenbaum Hebrew Academy at seven twenty-five. Immediately, Avishai noticed people staring. Conversations stopped. The regular chatter of schoolchildren had been replaced by an eerie silence, and Noah and Avishai were suddenly front and center. Unused to the attention, Avishai stood, frozen awkwardly by Noah's side. As they peered around, they were met with looks ranging from hateful glares to amused grins. Avishai took a deep breath and shuffled closer to Noah.

Just then, the principal, Dr. Cohen, walked by, and everyone turned away or lowered their gaze. Avishai tried to step away, to pass into the crowd, but the principal saw him before he was able to.

"Miller," Dr. Cohen's voice rang out.

"Good morning, Dr. Cohen. I, uh..." But before he could think of an excuse for the congregation of the majority of the student body, he was interrupted.

"Save it, boy," Dr. Cohen snapped. "You," he pointed to Noah, "and you," he said, turning back to point at Avishai. "In my office, this instant." The crowd started to "ooh" but a stern look from Dr. Cohen dispersed them almost immediately.

Avishai and Noah, now trembling, walked back to the principal's office with Dr. Cohen leading the way. Avishai looked to Noah for help, and was reassured by a kind nod. "We'll be okay," he whispered into Avishai's ear, then abruptly turned away from him thanks to a thoroughly disapproving look from Dr. Cohen.

The three walked into the office one at a time, with Avishai going in last. Even as he did, he was hesitant. It was as if his body didn't want to move. It locked into place for a moment, but he convinced himself to journey on into the principal's office.

They stood awkwardly for a moment as Dr. Cohen sat down behind his oak desk. He positioned his swivel computer chair so that he faced both of them at once, then motioned for them to take a seat.

"Well," he began once they'd sat, albeit uncomfortably, in the hard office chairs. Avishai squirmed to make himself more comfortable, but it was a vain attempt.

"You may not understand, but you two have placed me in quite the predicament. You see, boys, your parents pay a tuition so that you can attend this fine educational establishment." *Great,* Avishai thought. Already it was sounding condescending. "They pay good money, even though for some it can pinch the wallet to send their kids here, but parents do it anyway. Do you know why that is?"

They glanced at each other; Avishai could see the same uncertainty he felt reflected in Noah, and the two of them stayed silent.

"It's because we are an outstanding school with outstanding academics and outstanding ethics. We live our lives by the Torah, and that is why parents send their kids here. A lot of parents are willing to make sacrifices for their children to make sure they lead good, upstanding lives. The problem is, homosexuality isn't a part of that. Noah, I've reached out to your parents, but they want nothing to do with this, and Avishai, your father's office hasn't returned any of our calls. So here's what I have to offer you: If you can take back your statement and say that you were just confused or mistaken, then we can keep you at this school. Okay?"

Avsiahi stifled a laugh and looked at Noah with disbelief. Was he serious? "This isn't something we can just take back. I mean, we were telling the truth yesterday. On top of that, why would anyone believe we went through all that if it wasn't true?"

"Also, it's true," Noah reminded the principal. "We aren't going to just say that we changed our minds or anything. We're the same people, so you calling us in here doesn't change anything."

"Look," the principal said, throwing his hands in the air. "Noah, you're a great student. And Avishai, you're a good kid and your dad helps us financially. But I have to look at the bigger picture here, which includes a dozen parents calling to say that either you go or their children go. And some of them are also big funders. I don't really have a choice here." He fidgeted with the things on his desk, rubbing a pen between his thumb and forefinger. When Avishai looked up from the pen to his principal's eyes, he noticed Dr. Cohen couldn't meet his gaze.

"What does that even mean," Avishai asked, his fists clenching and his face reddening. "What do you mean you don't have a choice?"

"You need to leave. For now, at least. You can either retract your statement or you can wait for

the board to figure out what to do about all this."
He motioned around the room with both hands.

Avishai looked to Noah and saw the same
nervousness he was doing his best to choke down.
He couldn't manage to utter a single word. He
wasn't surprised at all that they were being
threatened with expulsion—in fact, that was one
of his only certainties in all of this. But he felt
himself growing more outraged as Dr. Cohen
continued to speak with complete disregard for
them.

"We will meet with our board of directors for
an emergency session tomorrow night. You may
come to speak on your behalf, and your parents
are also welcome." He glared at them, and Avishai
thought he saw a hint of regret in his eyes as he
said, "Until then, my hands are tied. I have no
choice but to insist that you leave the school
immediately. You may return when the board
reaches their decision. If they decide to side with
the parents who have complained, then the two of
you will need to find schooling elsewhere. I'm
sorry to do this, but I have no choice. And I'm
especially sorry about this," he added.

What more could there possibly be? "What do you
mean, 'this'?" Avishai asked when he had finally
gotten his voice back in working order.

The principal waved his hand at the door of
his office, and Joel and Nathan, two of the school's
security guards, stepped inside.

"Gentlemen, would you please escort these

two out of the building and off school property?" Dr. Cohen looked back at them. "I really am sorry, boys, but for the time being, this truly is my only option. I'll hope for the best during the session tomorrow evening. All right, you may leave now."

In a state of stunned silence, Avishai and Noah, followed closely by the two security guards, were escorted out of the building. The crowd of students in the hallway and lobby parted for their party, and there wasn't a soul in attendance who didn't stop whatever they were doing—be it midsentence or midstep—and turn to stare at their unfortunate fellow classmates. The pair may as well have had scarlet A's painted on their fleece jackets.

Everyone gasped as Avishai took hold of Noah's hand, and again when Joel, the older of the two security guards, stepped in-between them and slapped their hands apart. Avishai teared up and felt his face run hot with embarrassment.

Never had he been so humiliated in his life, and just because that this school needed to turn a profit, needed to keep the parents—their *customers*—happy. He walked through the halls of a place where he had felt hatred present every day of the two years he'd spent there, and all in the supposed name of God.

He stopped suddenly. He looked around at the startled students and shouted, "This isn't wrong!" gesturing between himself and Noah. "What's wrong is *this*." And he pointed to the principal's office, to the second guard, who was getting closer to him. "What's wrong here is that in this society, in this religion, you're allowed to justify discrimination. This isn't policy, this is hatred and bigotry!"

The door to Dr. Cohen's office swung open, and he flew into the hall. "That's it!" he yelled. "Joel, Nathan, I don't care what you do, but get these students out of my school immediately. And you," he said, pointing a bony finger at Avishai. "Forget any support from me at that meeting. I may like your father, but you and he are not one in the same. You are disturbing the peace. I offered you two an easy solution and you refused, so you have lost your privilege to be at this school, and as of now the both of you are trespassing. Get out."

Joel took Avishai by the shoulder and dragged him backward out of the school with Noah running after them.

"What are you all doing standing here?" Dr. Cohen shouted at the other students who had gathered to watch the whole ordeal play out. "Show's over, get to class. Anyone who doesn't beat the bell there gets to spend all day with me in in-school suspension. Now scram!"

The last thing that Avishai heard as he was pushed out the door was the thunder of hundreds of feet and the hushed whispers of stunned students as they rushed off to class before the bell sounded.

CHAPTER NINE

Avishai and Noah sat in the car for a while. Avishai certainly wasn't ready to go home, and he didn't think Noah was either. In the car they were in limbo, but once they were home, they would be faced with reality and would have to talk about what had happened. They would have to figure out what to do, and what to say when they went to the meeting the next night.

They would need to face the possibility of finding a new school. Avishai didn't even know how to start going about doing that. Especially without the necessary help and support of their parents. His dad would want him to go to a private school, and RHA was the only Jewish one in the area. Noah would have to decide what to do, too, but based on his dad's statement from the day before, maybe he would be willing to help.

Then Avishai remembered. "Oh, shit."

Noah looked back at him. "Ooshy, what's the matter?"

"No, I just—" He shook his head, laughing. "I just realized that I'm going to have to explain all of this to my dad, getting kicked out of school and everything. He's gonna be pissed." Noah was silent for a moment, looking down at his hands.

The laughter had stopped.

"Maybe it'll be okay," Noah said, still looking down at his hands. "He probably knew that coming out like this would entail some form of punishment from the school. I mean, it's pretty clearly one of their policies to send kids to JONAH, so…" Noah trailed off, sounding defeated.

Avishai brushed his finger on Noah's cheek, which caused him to look up and at him. "We should leave, Noni," Avishai said, suddenly feeling like there was a very heavy weight resting on his shoulders. He needed to go home and call his dad.

"Okay, Ooshy. But thinking about it, we really should call your dad when we get back," he said as he started the ignition.

They drove back in silence, but Avishai couldn't help but wonder if Noah was thinking about his parents and sister. Things had ended badly with his parents, but his sister… It had been different with Hadar. She didn't care that Noah was with Avishai. She loved him just the same. His parents should still love him, but they didn't. She did. Would her parents let Noah be a part of her life?

She was acting as the adult there, but she was still being punished. Sure, she didn't get to make the decisions in her house, but she had to suffer the consequences all the same. Her brother, whom she loved, who was her best friend, was just gone from her life entirely. How was that fair?

It was her parents' fault. They'd forced Noah to leave their home. It was child abuse. With no way of getting to Avishai's house to see her brother, and Noah not allowed to go either to his home or to their school to see her, they were separated entirely aside from phone calls.

Avishai literally couldn't imagine. How could he, really? He had lost his mother, but he'd known about that for a while. He'd known it was coming, and he'd been prepared by his mother, his father, and the hospice worker, once it had been deemed that his mother's cancer was untreatable.

His father was different. Yes, they'd grown distant, but at least Avishai had him. He was there if he actually needed him. He let Avishai continue live in his home, even though they were so different, and even though Avishai had lied to him about Noah. He did what he was supposed to—he acted as a parent. He helped his child in the ways that he could. He provided for him.

Noah's parents had done the opposite. They were acting irresponsibly. What was worse was that Avishai knew it was eating away at Noah. He had never been able to open up about real things to Avishai. He had told him once that he didn't want to add so much emotional stress to Avishai's life. But this, Avishai knew, needed to be talked about. Suddenly not having your parents there for you was a terrifying idea.

And with being separated from Hadar the way

Noah had... Avishai had lost his mom, but parents and siblings were so different. The pain was similar, but not similar enough that he could understand what Noah was feeling. Especially with Hadar alive, and knowing that she was suffering from this too. Avishai wanted Noah to talk about it, but he didn't want to initiate the conversation. All he could do was wait.

~~*

When they arrived home, Avishai got out of the car to go inside, but Noah didn't. Avishai shut his door and headed up the driveway, but quickly realized Noah hadn't followed. He turned back and spotted Noah still sitting in the car, looking the way he had this morning, when Avishai had gone to wake him up: under so much stress, and with so little control over it all. He saw tears streaming down Noah's cheeks.

Avishai tapped lightly on the window, and Noah turned to him, startled. He wiped his face, looking frustrated.

Noah unlocked his door, and Avishai opened it, stepped in, and wrapped his arms around him.

He knew better than to say anything. He knew Noah didn't want that. The silence was horrible, and Avishai just hoped that his being there would make Noah feel better. Noah turned to face Avishai and curled up in his arms. Avishai could feel the tears that leaked from Noah's eyes and slid down his cheeks.

He stayed there with Noah in his arms for what seemed like hours. Avishai didn't want to move, to break the silence, to end the comfort. They stayed there in that car a long time, just breathing into each other. Then, Noah started.

"I love being Jewish," he began. The words broke the silence so suddenly that it caused Avishai to step back and look at Noah. "Will we be able to find a rabbi to marry us—to do a Jewish ceremony for us?" he asked. Avishai didn't know, of course, and was slightly confused by the question. He didn't know how to answer something he wasn't sure of himself. Even more than that, he couldn't bear to pretend like he did.

Noah kept going, obviously spilling out everything he'd been holding inside. "Can we belong to a traditional *shul?* I don't want to have to go to a Reform or Reconstructionist *shul* because we aren't allowed to attend anywhere else. And our kids, can they have a normal childhood? Will they love us the same? Will they resent us? Will they get picked on because of us? Can we send them to Jewish schools? Will what just happened to us happen to them, too? Can we even raise them to be Jewish? Send them to camp like my parents did for me? I mean, we've planned so much of our future, but we never considered these things. We talked about where we would live, how many kids we'd have, what their names would be, but how come we never thought about these things?" By this point, tears were once again streaming down Noah's cheeks as his body was wracked with sobs.

Tears started to spring into Avishai's eyes, too, just from looking at Noah.

Noah pressed the heels of his hands against his eyes. "This isn't fair!" he yelled, sadness replaced by anger. "None of this is. Jacob and Leah can let people know that they're dating, and so can Jeremy and Sarah, all of them can! They can go to each other's houses for Shabbat dinner, or go out on dates. They can get married when they grow up, if that's what they want. They can go to Orthodox *shuls* and have a Jewish family and send their kids to nice Jewish day schools and Jewish camps and not have to worry about all of this...all of this extra shit. They're so lucky and they don't even realize! I'm so jealous of all they take for granted."

Avishai could say nothing to comfort him. He had all of the same concerns, and there was no way of knowing what to do about it or what their future could hold.

And of course none of this was fair. Of course he resented, even hated the other couples at their school. But there was nothing that he could do, and nothing that he could say, not in that moment, in that car, to be able to comfort Noah. He was right, maybe even entitled, to feel this way. Avishai knew he was.

So he did the only thing that he could think of.

He wrapped his arms around Noah again, and held him while the tears streamed down. They both cried, suddenly faced with the realization of what their life might be like—that it wouldn't be as perfect as they had always planned.

~~*

Once Noah had calmed down, they headed inside. They split up in the kitchen, Noah mumbling something about going to take a shower, and Avishai grabbing his cell phone to call his father. As he dialed, his mind told him to stop between every number, but he knew they had to talk.

The phone rang twice before his dad picked up.

"Hello?" he answered, seeming somewhat irritated.

"Dad, it's me," Avishai began. He wasn't sure how to start. He wasn't sure what to say. How could he begin to approach the subject of school?

"Hey, kiddo, good job at the press conference. You handled it well. I think my statement of support was well received, too. I'm sorry that I haven't called yet, I've just been so busy that I..."

But Avishai cut him off. "Dad, they kicked us out of school."

"*What?* What did the two of you do?"

"Nothing! We got to school, and Dr. Cohen called us into his office. He told us that parents had been complaining about me and Noah. He said that the parents, especially of the middle schoolers, were concerned that we would have a negative influence on their kids. Then he started saying that we would show them that it's okay to behave 'in a perverse and immoral manner' or some such BS.

"Then he looked at us and tried to be all good educator on us. He was just like 'on the other hand, you are both tuition-paying students, and we are an educational institute, so we're in a way obligated to teach young, especially confused minds that need guidance.' Then he kept listing all these pros and cons, and it's like he just wants to get the most money for the school. It was complete BS." Avishai sighed, frustrated and waiting for his dad to interrupt. When he didn't, Avishai continued.

"So finally he starts to explain that we have to leave, that we can't be at the school anymore. He said that the board of directors is going to have an emergency session tomorrow night to see if they should let us continue to be students there. Then he had two freakin' security guards escort us out of the building."

His dad remained silent.

"Dad, I don't know what to do! If we get kicked out, we have to find another school. And Noah's parents, they won't do anything. Dr. Cohen says we can go to the meeting tomorrow night, but what are we supposed to do? I mean, all we can do is say what they already know and hate."

"They have the right," his dad began, "to kick you out, because they are a privately owned educational institute, but this is still discrimination. Are parents allowed to go to the meeting tomorrow?"

Avishai was shocked. "Yeah, but I'm not sure what you can..."

This time, his dad cut him off. "Avishai, I'm a lawyer. This is undoubtedly discrimination. If need be, we will take this to court, but they can't do this. I'll come home. I'll be there by tomorrow night. I'm going to that meeting. I'll defend you. Good-bye. I'll see you tomorrow. I love you, Avishai."

"I love you too, Dad. I'll see you tomorrow." Avishai hung up with shaking fingers. He was amazed at his father's gesture. He had been so afraid for so long that his father would reject him, but it seemed like this had worked out well. He hung up the phone and fell into one of the kitchen chairs, his nerves frayed after the conversation with his father.

Noah reappeared from the bathroom, looking concerned. "What happened?" he asked frantically. "Is he letting me stay? Is he upset about school? Ooshy, talk to me."

"He is okay with you staying here. He doesn't want you to be homeless. He cares about you, about us, I think. I told him about school, and about what happened with Dr. Cohen. He said that they can kick us out, but that it's discrimination. It's kind of ironic, you know, because he always votes against LGBT discrimination bills, but I guess this is bigger than that. He's really into stepping up for your family, so maybe that's what this is to him."

"So what did he say about school, other than that they can, but at the same time can't, do what they're trying to do to us?"

"I'm not entirely sure what he's thinking, but he's coming back home. He's gonna fly in for the meeting tomorrow night. I mean, he is a politician, but before that he was an assistant district attorney. He even said that if need be, he will take this to court. It sounds just a little ridiculous, but, I mean, he's supporting us. He keeps saying that he's not okay with it, but I think he's coming around. What do you think, Noni?" he asked, but when he looked up, Noah was crying again.

"Noah, baby, what's the matter?"

"I'm so sorry," Noah began.

"What are you sorry for?" Avishai asked.

"I just, I feel like I did this all, like I set everything into motion by wanting to come out. I was the one who insisted that we tell someone, and I didn't deny it when Hadar asked if you were my boyfriend. I was the one who told you to use my name in that press conference. I started the relationship, I'm the reason we had to come out today, because of the relationship I started with you. All of this is my fault. Can you ever forgive me, Ooshy?"

"Forgive you?" Avishai asked, laughing and wiping the tears from Noah's cheeks. "Do you think I didn't want to tell people about us, about this? I did, I was just so scared. You don't think that I've wanted to shout it from the rooftops every day that we've been together? Do you think that I could have lied to someone if they'd asked if we were together? Especially a sibling, if I had one? Obviously not. Although I was a little concerned at first, I was thrilled Hadar knew. I was so happy to finally have someone to talk to."

He smiled, thinking back to Hadar. She had helped them feel like everything would be fine, but now it felt like forever ago that they'd had that little conversation in Noah's study room. He felt himself getting lost in his train of thought. He shook himself out of it. Noah needed him.

"Anyway, my love, anything to do with the press conference is my fault and Dad's. He's a jerk for making me into one of his political operatives," he said, shrugging it off like it was nothing. "Seriously, don't blame yourself. For any of this. None of it is your fault, and if we each hadn't done exactly what we did, we would still be here. And yeah, here sucks a little bit right now, but we're happy and together, and that's all that really matters in the end, right?"

By the time he'd finished, Avishai had tears welling in his eyes. He grabbed Noah and held him tight as he gave him a kiss. "I love you, Noni, and I always will. Never regret anything."

Noah wiped tears from his cheeks. "I love you too, Ooshy. Thank you for making me remember why."

~~*

When his dad came home that evening from the airport at precisely five thirty that night, just hours before the meeting, Avishai and Noah were going over possible responses to the questions his dad's press team had said the board members might ask or accusations they might pose. Claudia had stayed in DC, but was constantly texting them suggestions and reminders.

A cold shiver ran through Avishai's body as he heard his dad's keys jingling outside the door. Noah met his panicked eyes briefly as they jumped out of their seats to greet his dad. Noah was the first to reach him and, nervously, took Avishai's dad's advice by standing up straight and speaking loudly and clearly.

"Congressman Miller," he began. "Thank you so much, sir, for your kind words at the press conference, and for letting me stay here." He held out his hand as he held Avishai's father's gaze.

Avishai's dad looked at that hand, then shook it briefly.

"There's no need to call me sir, son." He smiled. "I'm so sorry to hear about what your parents did.

It's despicable and I am absolutely mortified that parents do this. After what I saw in the press conference, the way you maintained your composure in such a stressful situation, especially under the circumstances...well, I'm glad to see my kid has good taste."

He turned to Avishai. "Come on, give your father a welcome-home hug."

Avishai walked up to his father slowly and welcomed him back with a firm handshake. "Welcome home, Dad. How was your flight?"

His dad gave Avishai a small pat on the back after taking his hand back. "Wasn't too bad," he said. "Hey, kid, I'm proud of you, and I mean it. You too, Noah. You two boys did a great job with the conference and all those reporters. You made me proud, but more than that you didn't make fools of yourselves or of me. You two holding hands was very sweet. I'm sure that you guys are going to do fine tonight. No hand-holding, though. Somehow I don't think that that sort of thing would go over too great with the board."

Avishai frowned when his dad wasn't looking. His father was never like this. He had always been very distant and formal with Avishai. Why was he acting this way now, with him knowing that his child was gay, which he had always said he never supported? Then it occurred to Avishai: Noah was there. This wasn't his real father—or it wasn't his real personality, at least. He was just getting to know Noah. This was a meet and greet, a get to know you, this was campaigning.

"So," his dad began after they'd set aside the greetings and pleasantries. "Let's talk strategy, boys. Have you been prepping yet?" Nods from both of them. Of course they had been preparing. They were mature; they could take responsibility.

"Good," his dad said after they had both answered in the affirmative. "Just a little pointer that goes a long way with professional types: no nodding. That goes with the whole clear communication thing. There will be no nodding or shaking of your heads. There will be no shrugging, for that matter, either. If you have an answer, give it verbally. It cuts down on confusion and miscommunication. Don't answer anything that you deem too personal or at all slanderous. Wait to give all responses until you've thought them through clearly. Don't say anything more than necessary, and for the sake of all that is holy sit up straight and speak loudly and clearly. That will make for a good first impression and a lasting image. You don't want them to think you two are slobs who can't speak and haven't been taught basic table manners."

This is more his style. His dad was back to his normal, demanding self, because of course he was.

"All right, to get started, I am going to give you some practice questions they are probably going to ask." He gestured for them to move to the couch, and when they were all sitting, he leaned forward, pinning them with a look. "What are you going to say if they ask you about the Jewish morals and ethics surrounding homosexuality in the Torah?"

Avishai was first to speak. "Well, to start out with, I think that I would say to them that homosexuality is only one of thousands of subjects spoken about in the Torah. It is mentioned along with many things that, this day and age, are considered to be outdated and therefore moot to some extent." He looked at his father for a moment to gauge his response. The look on his dad's face told Avishai he was wrong.

"Okay then, good start," he said, and then dove into explaining how to do it all better.

After a few more practice questions, his dad looked at his watch. "All right, guys. It's getting close to game time. We should get going, don't you think? There might be traffic, and tardiness never makes for a good first impression."

With every moment as it ticked by, Avishai grew more and more nervous. They neared the RHA campus. He had never seen it before at night, and it appeared quite ominous and foreboding in the darkness. Although he had no idea what the outcome of that night's meeting would be, he knew that it would change his life forever.

CHAPTER TEN

They walked out of the brisk night air and into the school building. Avishai stayed on his dad's heels, barely aware of the hallways passing around him. He was shaking, and nausea rolled in his stomach as his dad opened the door to the boardroom and headed inside. Even without anyone else there—they were fifteen minutes early and Jews always run late—the dank, dungeon-like room felt judgmental, intimidating.

Several minutes after they'd entered the room, Dr. Cohen walked through the door. Following closely behind him were two of the three assistant principals, Mr. Stein and Mrs. Goldberg.

"That's Mrs. Goldberg," Avishai explained to his dad, pointing to her. He knew his dad had met these people at the gala that the school held every year for the top donors, but doubted he would have remembered any of them. "That's Mr. Stein, the one who used to be a math teacher. I never had him and neither did Noah. The last one is Mr. Klein. Noah had him and so did Hadar, and I think he's on our side, he really liked the two of them."

His dad just nodded.

Mr. Klein walked in just before the meeting

started, a stack of quizzes under his arm. He smiled in the general direction of Noah, Avishai, and his dad, but turned away quickly after meeting the disapproving gaze of Mr. Stein. Then, at seven thirty on the dot, the entire board, all men clad in black suits, marched into the room together, apparently having been deliberating in an adjoining room for some time prior to the meeting.

Although there were very few, some parents did attend. They sat in the same area as Noah, Avishai and his dad. The administrators and board members sat around a long table, and everyone else present sat in fold-up chairs set out near the back of the room.

Mr. Spitzer, the chairman of the board, was the one who called the meeting to order. Avishai didn't know why this guy was chairman; he didn't have any kids at the Academy and from what the other students said, all he did was donate a lot of money to the school. Maybe that was all it took sometimes.

Mr. Spitzer tapped a small gavel twice on the table in front of him before welcoming people the meeting and startling Avishai back to reality.

"The Board of the Rosenbaum Hebrew Academy has been faced," he began, speaking slowly into his microphone, "with a difficult dilemma. As many of you may know, we are privileged here to teach many students, one of whom is the son of the congressman of the

Seventh District of Georgia. Due to his role in our community, Avishai Miller felt it necessary to publicly come out as a homosexual on Monday of this week, along with his boyfriend Noah Benowitz, who is also a student here. The board would like to start off by saying that we do not support this behavior."

Avishai felt himself blush, and slunk down in his seat a little. He had always hated the term "homosexual;" it sounded like a diagnosis. Tonight it felt like a criminal charge.

"As Jews, we must live by the Torah, and by the word of God. These lead us quite clearly to the conclusion that homosexuality is wrong. We will not stand to have our young children's minds contaminated, corrupted, and molded by this perverse and disgusting influence. Their way of thinking and of living differs greatly from our own as normal, healthy, moral Jews."

Avishai clenched his hands, anger burning in his chest. There was nothing wrong with him or with Noah. They were normal *and* healthy *and* moral. He was furious that this man thought he had the right to tell him that what and who he was was wrong. He prayed every day, kept kosher, celebrated all the holidays and observed Shabbat—how many other students could say the same? How many faculty members, for that matter? Or even board members? Yet he and Noah were the ones facing expulsion.

"It is the opinion of this board that in order to

maintain the stasis that our school has reached, we must not stand for this type of behavior. We must rid our school of this influence and keep the other students away from the misconception that this sort of thing is appropriate. We have found in our deliberation that these two students, Avishai Miller and Noah Benowitz, must be removed from our school."

Avishai's breath caught in his chest. He tried to look straight ahead so as not to see the look on his dad's face or on Noah's. He had known this was a possibility, and a likely one, at that, but he had never accepted that it could actually happen. Avishai stopped listening to anything but the roaring in his ears, but he snapped back to attention when Mr. Spitzer said, "We suggest that they attend the JONAH program. Past students at this learning establishment have found great success and guidance in this program, as well as with certain psychiatric specialists. Although we do not require that these students seek help, it has been determined that these students will need to be cleared by a psychiatrist of the school's choosing before they will be allowed to be admitted back into our school."

Conversion therapy. No way in hell was Avishai going to put up with that. It didn't matter if they would let him back in the school; it wasn't worth it. And he would lose Noah.

Mr. Spitzer continued, "This is not a punishment for these two students, but rather a reflection of Jewish values and how our school has decided to deal with certain circumstances as they come up in today's adjusting society."

Avishai stared daggers ahead at Mr. Spitzer.

"We hope that the students whose actions brought this meeting to session this evening, Avishai Miller and Noah Benowitz, realize the errors of their ways and are able to be cured and rejoin our school community at some point in the future. Until then, this meeting is adjourned. Thank you all and have a nice night."

"Hey!" Noah shouted, standing to address the whole room. "There's nothing wrong with us! We deserve to be here! And you said we could talk at the meeting!" he yelled at Dr. Cohen, who chose this moment to look down and examine his shoes.

"The board guaranteed no such thing," Mr. Spitzer assured the crowd. "And even if we had, it doesn't matter, because we have school precedent for the disciplinary actions we are taking. I'm sorry, Mr. Benowitz, but I'm going to have to ask you to leave."

Just then, the two security guards from school, Joel and Nathan, appeared once more in the doorway. Avishai had flashbacks of being dragged out of the school and, deciding against going through that again, walked slowly to the door. A glance told him Noah and his father were following. He felt like the Biblical figure Lot, leaving his hometown while it was being destroyed. He didn't look back at the room, for fear of being turned into a pillar of salt—the fate that had befallen Lot's wife when she'd looked back at Sodom. They had to face forward.

~~*

The ride home from the board meeting was stressful and silent. The meeting had only been a few minutes in length, so Avishai was pretty sure that the part they had been present for was just for show. The real meeting had taken place long before Avishai and Noah had arrived at the school, and their fates had already been decided when they'd stepped into the boardroom. They'd been made to believe they would have the opportunity to defend themselves, to change the minds of the board members. But they hadn't.

They'd been tricked—and all the work that they had each put in preparation for that night had all along been a waste of time.

As they all three arrived home, Avishai knew that they had to have a conversation about what had happened, but it was difficult to get the words flowing. Noah was the first to break the silence.

"Those bastards!" he shouted as soon as the front door was closed. "We fell for it. None of them did anything but nod along with Dr. Cohen and Mr. Spitzer. What on earth or in heaven gives either one of them the right to do any of this? What gives those two the freakin' right to interpret God, to interpret the Torah, to say that they forbid homosexuality and that they want to run their school accordingly?"

Avishai and his dad were both quiet, which for Avishai was rare when he was with Noah. After the initial burst of anger, Noah paced silently around the dimly lit living room. Avishai couldn't do anything except play and replay the night's frightful end over and over. He watched the smarmy board members and their reactions in his mind and could even see them on the backs of his eyelids when he closed his eyes. He thought about sitting down on a couch in the living room but felt too anxious to be still.

He toed his shoes off and made for the stairs, too numb and exhausted to explain to Noah and his dad where he was going or why. They let him go. He wandered to his room and laid down on the bed. It felt like his life was over. He wasn't even crying now, just sort of accepting that his life was ruined. He stared up at the glow-in-the-dark stars his mom had long ago painted on the ceiling and prayed to God that he would get through this, because it truly felt like he wouldn't. He thought about his mom, how disappointed she would be if he hurt himself. She had been so strong when she was diagnosed, and had fought so hard. Why had she died, but he was still alive?

It just didn't make sense.

He closed his tired eyes, and when he next opened them it was morning, and the light was peeking in from behind the curtains. He felt better than he had the night before, and was thankful for that, at least.

~~*

He walked down the stairs quietly before realizing that both his dad and Noah were already awake and at the breakfast table, so he didn't need to be quiet.

He looked at the clock that hung on the wall of the kitchen. It was eight in the morning, the time that classes started at the Academy. He thought about his classmates, and wondered what they would be doing in English, his first-period class. "Hey," he said to the room. He received a smile from Noah and a nod from his father but that was all. After another moment, he tried again. "Um, what are we going to do about school?" he asked tentatively. "I mean, we need to keep going to school, right? We don't have any other options in terms of Jewish day schools, and I'm pretty sure Catholic schools wouldn't have the warmest welcome for the two of us. I mean, of course, there's also public school, but I don't know how well me going back to one would work out..."

"No, you're right," his dad chimed in. "Public school wouldn't necessarily be the best option for you guys. The students there can be so cruel, and they don't care about their education as much because they're getting it for free, they don't need to apply themselves because if they don't, then it's at no loss to themselves or their parents. The teachers get paid a shit salary, so they don't work as hard. I won't have you two go to a school like that."

Avishai knew that what the congressman was saying was total bull—that public schools and their students could be as good as or even better than private schools. His dad had always complained about such stupid things. But he also knew that he was under a lot of stress and picking a fight about public education would have to wait for a less urgent time.

"Well," he said. "I don't really think that there is anything else. We've pretty much exhausted our options. I mean, we need a private school, but we've been kicked out of the Jewish one, and I don't think there are any secular ones in the area, so..."

"Actually," Noah said, suddenly picking up his head. "There is another school. I read about it in some research I did a few weeks ago when we decided to come out, as a just-in-case backup plan, and then I searched them up again last night. It's called the Rainbow Alternative School, and it's around an hour from here. I know it's far, but it's a school for kids, generally, that have been having trouble with bullying at their school because they're gay. I know that isn't our situation exactly, but I'm pretty sure that they could help us."

"That might work, actually," Avishai chimed

in, excited but unsure. "I've heard about it too. I saw a Tumblr post about it. I didn't know they had one in Georgia, so I didn't look into it. If you guys think that this could work, then I can look it up and we can find some info on it." When Noah and his dad nodded, Avishai took out his phone and Googled it.

He skimmed the information given on the site and read it aloud. "Pretty much it says that it is a nonjudgmental environment for middle through high school students who are lesbian, gay, bisexual, or transgender. They have zero tolerance for bullies, open enrollment, and it looks like their tuition actually isn't outrageous. It's a lot less than the tuition is over at RHA. Do you want me to write down the number for you to call, Dad?" When his father nodded, Avishai ran to get a pen and some paper to write the name of the school, the address of their campus, and finally their phone number so he could call.

"Did you happen to notice," his dad asked, after he'd retrieved the paper and recorded the school's information, "if they offer any financial aid or scholarship opportunities?"

Avishai paused for a moment and looked back at the website. "Uh, yeah, they offer merit-based scholarships and need-based financial aid, but why? It's actually less than the tuition was at RHA, so I don't think that..."

His father cut him off midsentence. "Keep in mind, Avishai, I am now paying for two students." He gestured at Noah, sitting in the corner of the room.

"No, that's okay," Noah said. "I have some money from my Bar Mitzvah and from birthdays, and I can probably get a pretty good merit-based scholarship, so..."

"Nonsense," Avishai's father insisted. "While you live here, you will be treated no differently than Avishai. That money should be going to college savings. Parents are supposed to take care of schooling costs before that point. Also, your parents probably have complete control of your bank account. Sorry to be worst case scenario man, but I don't think they would kick out their only son and then hand him his life's savings."

"Oh, I…" Noah started. "I guess I just hadn't thought about that. You're probably right." He hung his head Avishai put a comforting hand on his shoulder.

"Why don't I give the two of you a moment?" Avishai's dad asked. Noah nodded glumly as he watched him stand up and leave the table. Avishai was about to say something to Noah, but just then Noah's phone chimed. Noah looked over at it and after a minute he smiled to himself.

"Okay, well, I'm still broke," he said through a sad smile. "But Jeremy just messaged me, and the guys still want to hang out this weekend, so I guess my life's not totally over!" The three of them laughed, but Avishai was uncomfortable—"the guys" were a group of boys who had never been particularly nice to him. They were led, of course, by Jeremy and his crew. They were popular and friends with Noah and represented everything Avishai didn't have. No one was texting him to say they were going to stick by his side through all of this. He probably didn't have close enough friends at school to warrant that amount of attention. His constant depression and low energy had made it impossible to get close to anyone. Except Noah, that was.

Noah must have sensed that something was wrong, because he looked up and said brightly, "You should come too, the guys said they want to meet you."

Avishai looked away, embarrassed. "They already know me," he said glumly.

"They know you as that quiet kid. They don't know you as my boyfriend. They want to get to know you for real." His smile told Avishai this was true, but he still wasn't sure. These kids had never had any interest in being his friend before, so why now?

"I don't have to come with you," he said finally. "I don't want to cramp your style or be somewhere I'm not wanted. I get it, I wasn't popular before, so I probably won't be now. I'm just that quiet kid no one knows."

"Hey!" Noah snapped. "You're more than that. You're more than all of this, everything that's going on. You're a real person with a real life, you're not just some school trope. And even if you were, I'm right here with you waving the rainbow flag." He kissed Avishai on the cheek and tussled his hair.

Avishai still wasn't satisfied, though. "You don't have to pretend I'm just one of the guys," he said. "I know I'm not like them, and that you hang out with them for different reasons than you hang out with me. I don't want to cause a rift in the group because—"

Noah cut him off. "Read the stupid text," he said, waving his phone in Avishai's face. Once Avishai's eyes focused, he read the message: *Congrats on the whole gay thing, bring the bf to James' house Saturday night so we can all meet him.*

Avishai laughed a little in spite of himself. "I'm sorry," he admitted. "I'm just not used to people wanting to be around me, or get to know me. I just assumed I wasn't wanted."

Noah smiled sadly. "You always think that," he told Avishai. "You think that no one wants you around, but you're actually super cool and interesting and people want to get to know you better. You need to have a little more faith in people and a lot more faith in yourself. I want you to meet my friends, they want to meet you, so let's do this. And if you hate them, there will be hundreds of other kids at this new school that you can make friends with. Okay?"

Avishai nodded once more. "Dad," he called. "Come on, let's call the school."

His father walked in with his cell phone and

nodded confidently at Noah and Avishai. Avishai wished he could steal that confidence for this new school, if they ended up there, but knew he could only ever be who he was. Maybe kids at this new school would take more nicely to a shy choir kid. He hoped so, at least.

CHAPTER ELEVEN

Noah dialed the Rainbow Alliance Alternative School and put it on speakerphone so they could all hear and speak. It rang only two times before someone picked up on the other side. "Rainbow Alliance Alternative School, how may I help you?" A knot rose in Avishai's stomach, and he twisted his fingers together, staring at the phone.

"Uh, hi, yes," his dad responded after a moment of silence. "My name is Congressman Daniel Miller. I have two students who are very interested in applying. My son and his boyfriend, who are now both under my care, were expelled from their school, the Rosenbaum Hebrew Academy, after my son made a public statement regarding his sexuality. I wanted to find out if it would be possible to enroll the two of them for the remainder of this year."

"Well—" she started to say before Avishai's dad cut her off.

"May I speak to your principal, please? I understand that registrations and entrance testing and processing can take a while, but over here on this end, we'd rather have this whole thing all sorted out and taken care of as quickly as possible."

Avishai was sweating and rocking in place. He bit at his lower lip as he waited for what seemed like an eternity for the woman to respond.

He breathed a sigh of relief as he heard shuffling and what sounded like a keyboard clacking on the other side of the phone. "All right," she said finally. "Unfortunately, Dr. Blas is unavailable at the moment. He has a meeting until eleven, and I'll have him call you back just as soon as I can, but if you'd like to get started with the application process, I can email you the first part right now."

Avishai's dad rattled off his email, and so their application process began. After each of them had opened their laptops, they went through their applications as quickly as they could, with Avishai's dad staring over their shoulders and pacing while they worked. This school was literally their last resort, and Avishai wanted to get these applications filled out and handed back in as soon he could. He really did want to get all of this behind him, and assumed that Noah did too, especially considering how important Noah's education was to him. They had already missed three days of school, and who knew how long this whole process could take?

The questions asked on the application were just general background questions, things about where the applicant had lived, grown up, and what schools they had attended. Then it asked why the applicant was leaving their former school. It didn't take too long to fill in all of the answers. Noah and Avishai had just emailed the last of the medical forms, which, thank goodness, Noah had access to a digital copy of, when Avishai's dad's phone rang.

"Go upstairs, boys," his dad said, picking it up and waiting with his thumb over the Answer button. "I'd like to talk to him alone."

Avishai exchanged a look with Noah, and the two of them headed upstairs, only to pick up the phone in the hallway outside Avishai's room so they could listen in. Avishai was worried his dad would try to use his power or money to influence the school like he had with Rosenbaum, but at the same time was so desperate to get in that he almost didn't care.

"Mr. Congressman," the principal was saying, "Mrs. Stouber filled me in on the details of your case. I'm so sorry to hear about what happened, especially after hearing about your son's brave coming out the other day. I am glad to see, though, that you've done the right and responsible thing and put personal and political differences behind you for the good of your child."

"Why thank you, Dr. Blas, but I need you to know that Avishai and Noah's schooling is of the utmost importance to myself and to them. They've already missed three days of school, so I'd like to get them into your school as soon as possible. Falling behind academically would only add to their stress. I'm sure that your school has dealt with similar situations before and has been able to accommodate them, am I right?"

Oh God, Avishai thought. This was when his dad was going to put on the pressure and intimidate the principal. It was like a car crash, and he couldn't look away. He didn't want to hear it, but he knew it was coming and couldn't ignore it.

"Mr. Congressman, if I may," Dr. Blas said. "Your political power should have nothing to do with this."

What? Avishai blinked, surprised.

"If it did, if you needed to manipulate a school to get what is only best for your son, should you really be sending him there?"

There was an awkward silence. Avsishai knew that his father hated being called out, but that was exactly what this man was doing. "I see your point, Dr. Blas," his dad finally, sounding slightly dejected.

"I'm glad you do, but, like you said, we are quite accustomed to doing what it takes to meet the needs, whatever they might be, of our students and of their parents. Many do like to have their children begin attending right away after leaving an old school. We can set you up for a tour of the campus grounds at..." He paused for a moment, probably checking the time or some schedule. "How does two p.m. today sound?" he asked.

"That sounds wonderful, thank you. Should

we meet in your office, or...?"

"My office is fine. I'll set up a student-led tour and will see you then."

After they'd ended the call, Avishai calmed slightly, his heart no longer going a mile a minute and his breathing beginning to deepen. He wiped his sweaty hands on his pants as his father called to them from downstairs.

They clunked down the stairs as quickly as they could and arrived in front of his dad.

"Yeah, Dad?" said Avishai, trying to play it cool. "Was that Dr. Blas?" Avishai could tell his dad was not at all fooled by his performance, and the strongly guilty look on Noah's face didn't help.

"Boys, I know that you two were listening in on the conversation. I could hear the two of you breathing. So, you know and understand what's going on, right?" They nodded, and Avishai was glad to not have to waste any time on listening to his dad repeat the contents of the phone call. "Good. So, go change into something appropriate, and we'll get going. Actually, Noah, what you're wearing should be fine. Avishai, hustle. We don't want to be late."

Avishai ran up to his room to change while his dad and Noah sat on the couch. Things were falling into place again, and he did his best to get ready as quickly as he could. When he came back downstairs, he was clad in a gray button-down tucked into a pair of black slacks.

"Ready to go?" he asked. They left, and Avishai was eager to get to the school. Maybe it would help bring this instability to an end.

CHAPTER TWELVE

As expected, the ride took around an hour. Avishai had decided to sit in the backseat with Noah, which meant his dad controlled the radio. He turned it to the classic rock station and then turned the volume all the way up. *Fair enough*, Avishai thought. He sat back and mentally prepared for meeting new people and being in a new environment. He felt himself growing anxious now and then, but tried to calm down with the knowledge that they had already been through some of the worst possible experiences; their luck had nowhere to go but up.

They arrived at the school's campus at around one forty-five, and used their extra few minutes getting lost on the way to the main office. Through the windows in the classroom doors, Avishai could see children learning. He felt strange, like he should be in the classes doing the same thing: sitting in those chairs, taking chemistry tests, or cramming for a vocab test during lunch. The halls were silent, since every student was in class.

One thing Avishai noticed struck him as odd. The majority of the students seemed to be either genderqueer or guys. Or both. There were very few feminine people here, and Avishai made a mental note to ask their guide.

They finally arrived at the main office only a few moments before their tour of the school was to start. They walked in and were greeted by Mrs. Stouber. She was a heavyset middle age woman, wearing a touch too much makeup, but she looked like someone easy to talk to, and that put him at ease. The office was filled with framed newspaper clippings about the school, along with pictures of smiling students at various local events. He wanted to be in one of those pictures.

Avishai's dad signed them in as he and Noah settled down in the seats in the office's waiting area. He joined them after a moment, toting three Visitor Pass stickers. At two o'clock exactly, they were called into the principal's office.

When they entered, they were greeted by a short, thin man with graying black hair. He was just throwing out the remnants of his lunch: an orange peel and what looked to be the wrappings of a schoolmade peanut butter and jelly sandwich. Some things were the same in any school.

"Good afternoon, it's a pleasure to meet all of you," said Dr. Blas as he extended a hand to each of them. "Please, have a seat," he said, gesturing to the couch and chairs that lined the walls of his office. Once they were seated, he continued. "Avishai, Noah, before we get down to business, I would just like to congratulate the two of you on coming out. I know that your school had a less than ideal reaction, and Noah, I'm sorry to hear about your parents, but this is still a monumental and quite freeing step, regardless of the outcome. Also, I'm sure that you've made it so much easier for any other LGBT kids in your school or in your community."

"We've reviewed your applications and all things are in order to get the two of you into a classroom by Monday. I'm sorry, you don't get to miss any more school on our account," he teased. Noah snickered, but Avishai got a little nervous. Things were moving so quickly. It was true he didn't want to miss any more school, but he hadn't even seen this place or met any of the students yet, and he was already in a position to commit.

"But first, I'd like to get to know the two of you—or, rather, all three of you, a little better. What sorts of things do you like to do?"

Noah spoke up first, breaking the awkward quiet. Avishai was glad to not have to be first, but really wished he didn't have to speak at all.

"Well, I spend a lot of time studying, honestly. I haven't this week, obviously, but usually I do. I've made high honor roll every marking period each year since I started getting number grades back in middle school. Back at RHA, I also did math team and I was in a bunch of instrumental performing groups. I play the French horn. Does this school have a band or orchestra or any other groups?" he asked eagerly.

"We've got a band, orchestra, jazz band, and then we've also got a pit orchestra for the spring musical," Dr. Blas said, smiling. "This year we're doing the musical *A Funny Thing Happened on the Way to the Forum*. We also have a math team, if you're interested in competing for our school."

"I'd love to play in the band, and depending on if they need a French horn, I'd also love to do orchestra and the other groups," Noah said. "But, well, I don't really like doing the math team. I did well because I'm good at math, but the only reason I did it was to make my parents happy. Now that I don't have to worry about them, I don't think that I will."

"Well, that's perfectly fine. I'm sure that Mr. Garelick, the music chairperson and director of the instrumental groups, would be thrilled to have you. And in terms of the math team, you shouldn't be doing anything that makes you unhappy. What a lot of kids realize, usually for the first time when they get here, is that they don't have to do anything for other people, even their parents. Do what you do to make yourself happy, not anyone else. Avishai, what about you?"

Avishai hesitated, unsure how to answer the without making himself sound bad, as he had never excelled at school. "Um, well, I guess that I would say I get decent grades. Nothing special, you know, but they aren't horrible. I get mainly B's with a few A's, sometimes some C's. I sang in the choir at school, but they didn't have a musical or anything. It was just the regular old concert choir. I don't know, I was never really into doing clubs." Avishai looked down at the floor, and kept his gaze there, even when he noticed that Noah was trying to make eye contact with him.

"All right, well, like I said, you don't have to do anything that you don't want to. We have some teachers and a student group here that do free tutoring in every subject, and we also have some programs and people who can help a lot with the college application process." Avishai's jaw unclenched. There was finally someone who didn't care that his grades weren't perfect, but was willing to work with him nonetheless.

"So, why do you want to attend? Mr. Congressman, why would you like to see your son and Noah as students here?"Avishai hesitated again. Sitting in that room, at that moment, he knew the answer: they had run out of options. He of course didn't want to give this answer, for fear of being denied acceptance. Once again, Noah was first to speak, and Avishai was thankful.

"I'll be honest with you, Dr. Blas. We have no other options. We have nowhere else to go, no one to turn to. On Sunday I was kicked out of my house, and then, on Tuesday, I was humiliated when I was 'escorted' by two armed guards out of RHA, which has been my second home for the past two years."

Avishai wasn't sure if Dr. Blas wanted Noah to continue but he certainly wanted him to, eager to hear what he had been thinking and thankful that he didn't have to speak yet.

"On Wednesday night, I was told that I was being expelled, regardless of the fact that I had done nothing wrong. The Rosenbaum Hebrew Academy is the only Jewish day school in the area, and that leaves Catholic schools, but we can't go there because they have the same attitude toward gay students as RHA does. We are not just applying here because this is our last chance, but because we need this. For the first time ever, we need people around us who are like us, who have been through what we've been through, who can give us support when we need it, and hopefully we can do the same for them. We like what this school stands for and we need what it can provide."

Dr. Blas smiled brightly at them. "Well, Mr. Benowitz, that was quite impressive. After speaking with you gentlemen, I believe you would both fit in quite nicely here, and I'm excited for you two to join our community. I'm going to have a student representative come and show you around, give you a little tour of the school. If you have any questions, feel free to ask her, or ask me after the tour. I'd be happy to help with." He rose to shake hands with them, then led them out the door.

"It was a pleasure to meet all three of you, Mr. Congressman, Noah, and Avishai. And I'm so glad all of this is working out, and for Noah, that something finally is. Best of luck to you all, and enjoy the tour."

~~*

Their tour guide arrived a few moments after the bell rang and introduced herself as Shelly Monderer. She was wearing a bright-pink T-shirt that that read CAUTION: Censorship Can Lead To Stupidity! National Banned Book Week 2012. She was also wearing jeans, black Converse with rainbow laces, and a huge smile. She was tall and willowy, easily taller than Avishai, and maybe even Noah. She greeted them with an outstretched hand.

Avishai's dad was the first to reach out for it. "Hi," he said. "It's nice to meet you, Shelly. My name is Congressman Daniel Miller. This is my son, Avishai, and this is his boyfriend, Noah."

"Nice to meet you all. Let's get started!" She led them out of the office and into the once again empty hallways. "So, this is the Rainbow Alliance Alternative School, and here we offer students the necessary environment to grow and thrive in, one where they are truly free to be themselves, and bullying is practically nonexistent. It does, unfortunately, still exist, but we do employ a zero tolerance policy for bullying of any sort, so mind your manners!" she called out jokingly to Avishai and Noah, who laughed nervously.

"All of our students are members of the LGBTQ – lesbian, gay, bisexual, trans, queer – community. Anyone need a term defined?" she asked cheerfully. They all shook their heads. Avishai, although he had never been exposed to any of this at home, had found Tumblr to be quite informative.

"All right, great. In terms of the teachers here, the majority are here because of the same reason that all of the students are: they've been fired or discriminated against because they happen to be LGBTQ. Some are not, they were just looking for a job, felt connected in some way to our mission statement, and were qualified and empathetic enough for the school. Not every teacher is, mind you. It takes a lot to get hired here, so you can know that all of your teachers are the best.

"So, if you'll follow me, I'll give you your tour. If anyone has any questions, please feel free to interrupt me at any point," she said sweetly.

Again, Noah was the first to speak. "This may sound sort of odd or rude," he began. Both Avishai and his dad eyed him suspiciously, but Shelly's expression remained eager. "I just, well, I noticed that there aren't that many cisgender girls here. I just wanted to know why that is."

She didn't look at all irritated by the question, but rather seemed quite prepared for it. "For starters, you may have noticed that the majority of the students here are in some way gender-variant. This is simply because they usually have the hardest time at other schools facing bullies, unaccepting administrations, and such.

"Our next largest group is cisgender gay or bi

boys, because they have the next largest instance of being bullied. Cisgender lesbian or bi girls generally have the lowest instances of being bullied at school, compared to other members of the LGBTQ community. Now, my very being here is proof that lesbians get bullied too, and this should not be misconstrued that it's in any way easier for queer girls, but we tend to face less ridicule as a whole, even though we too are met with a very low amount of tolerance and support, especially here in the South. Great question, by the way. Kids don't usually tend to notice the gender gap."

She led them to a wing that was painted light green with forest-green lockers. Avishai peered through the windows in the classroom doors.

"This is the green hallway, but I'm sure that you probably could have figured that by now," Shelly explained. We have all of our science classes down in this hall. We offer only one core subject per grade, but we also offer different levels. For freshmen we have regular earth science and honors earth science. Sophomores can take either regular, honors, or advanced placement Biology. For juniors—you guys are juniors, right?" When all three of them nodded, Shelly continued. "For juniors, we have the option of taking regular, honors, or advanced placement chemistry. You can choose whichever is right for you, and if you want we have some electives, like zoology."

She spoke as she walked, filling them in on

clubs, athletics, and other activities along the way. "Do you guys take languages at school?" she asked as they turned down another hallway, this one painted red.

"I took French from sixth grade to tenth, but I was never very good at it," Avishai said. "I had to go until sophomore year, but I quit after that. Noah's really good at Spanish, though."

Noah blushed deeply, from the base of his neck all through his face. Avishai loved to brag about how smart Noah was, especially when it came to languages.

"¿Hablas Español?" Shelly asked him, obviously excited.

"Sí," he responded quickly. *"Empezé a aprender Español cuando estaba un niño en Boston, en el cuarto grado. ¿Y tú?"*

Avishai didn't even try to understand what he had just said.

"Tu acento es fantástico," she exclaimed. "Anyway, this is the red hall. We have all of the language classes here. We offer French, Spanish, and Mandarin Chinese. All of our English classes and electives take place here, too. We have a state-based curriculum, same as any school has for English, and we also offer advanced placement English for eleventh graders and advanced placement English literature for our seniors. Electives include journalism, creative writing, and science fiction.

Avishai thought about how different this

school was from his old one. There, they'd been allowed no choices. Here it seemed freer, in more ways than one.

"For the other languages—well, I guess I'll just talk about Spanish. We offer levels one through five, and we offer advanced placement Spanish language for juniors and literature for seniors. I'm taking AP Spanish lit, and the teacher is great. We also have an entry-level class for all of our languages, in case you feel like picking a new one up or dusting off your French skills." She offered the last bit to Avishai, looking hopeful.

"Sorry," he said. "You don't know how badly I did in French, and I probably shouldn't subject another language to that abuse. Noah's been talking about taking up French, though, so..." Avishai smiled, watching Noah's flush return.

"I just thought that it might be useful," he said meekly. "I used to have this wonderful Spanish teacher who always said, 'Chances are, every one of you in this class will do one of the following: Marry someone from a different country, work in a different country, or work with or for people from a different country. Now you tell me that language isn't power.' He was great."

Shelly smiled gently at him and paused, perhaps trying to think of an equally insightful quip. Avishai assumed that she hadn't been able to bring one to mind when she led them out of the red hall and into the blue one. Based on the math team posters, Avishai assumed that this wing was the one dedicated to math.

They saw a few students walking in the hallways holding hall passes. Most waved at the three of them and almost every one of the students said hello to Shelly. Overall it seemed to be a pretty friendly crowd, which Avishai found encouraging.

They made it to the lobby and turned left into a yellow hall. Hung up on the walls were beautiful drawings and paintings, and just as beautiful were the clay sculptures and ceramic works which sat in display cases carved into the walls.

"This," Shelly said excitedly, "is the art wing. All of our visual art classes are held here. We offer all of the classes for any student who is interested in them. We've got basically any art class you could want. Over here," she said, gesturing around the halls to the artwork, "is some of the seniors' artwork, and this," she said, pointing to one of the beautiful pencil drawings, "is mine."

"This is my little sister, Arielle," she said, pointing to a drawing of a young girl watching the snow fall. We adopted her from Haiti when she was four, and this was the first time she had ever seen snow. She's nine, now. I just finished it in October, after working on it all through junior year. Her birthday is in January, so I'm taking it home for her as a tenth birthday present."

"She'll love it," Avishai said confidently. Noah nodded his agreement and they exited the hall and walked back toward the lobby.

They peeked through the office window and caught sight of Mrs. Stouber. She waved to them. They were on their way in another direction and off to the purple wing soon. Avishai was slightly perplexed by this hall. There were four doors, three on one wall and the fourth on the opposite side. They entered first into the first room on the side with three doors.

"This is the chorus room," Shelly said. The room was large but plain, aside from photographs of what looked like past concerts and shows the school had put on. There was a wall-long set of curved risers with chairs filling in all three rows.

Avishai took a closer look at some of the pictures, recognizing sets and costumes from a few musicals he was familiar with. Excitement rose in him at the idea of getting to perform in something as grand as a musical.

"In this room we have chorus and we rehearse for the musical. Are either one of you interested in that?" she asked.

Avishai shyly raised his hand.

"Finally!" she exclaimed. "We've found something that makes you excited! Chorus is an elective, and so is drama, which also meets in here. We'll start the casting and rehearsal process for the yearly musical in November and the shows will be for two weekends in March. We have a band, chorus, and orchestra concert right before the holiday break in December, and then one in February and one in June. You can probably learn the music quickly enough, if you want to perform in our next concert."

"Yeah," he said excitedly. "Actually, that sounds really great. Do you happen to know how many kids are in the chorus?"

"Hmm…I want to say this year we have thirty-eight kids, but don't quote me on it. Why do you ask?"

"No, it just, well, this is kind of a huge room and it looks like it could fit a couple hundred kids at least. I was just curious."

"Oh, well, that's only because we have all of the musical rehearsals in here, too. Most of the school participates in one way or another, whether it's as a part of the cast, the pit orchestra, tech and lighting, crew. There's something for everyone to do and it's really just so amazing when you see the final product, with all of the students having put their full efforts forward to make it the best that they can. We've got some really talented students here."

She let Avishai take another look around, then suggested, "Should we head back out?"

Avishai nodded and looked down at his watch. It was almost the end of the school day, but he wasn't sure whether or not their tour guide knew and thought that she might like to.

As Shelly pulled the door open, a middle-aged man on the other side dropped his hand from where he'd been turning the knob and took a surprised step back. Then he grinned and said,

"Shelly! Is this a tour? Are these new students to frighten away?" He winked at them, then held out a hand for all of them to shake. "Hello there, everyone. My name is Mr. Rattner. I teach the chorus here, I am the drama teacher, and I direct the theatre company. I also run voice lessons, so feel free to sell your soul to me now if you're interested in joining." He laughed, and soon Shelly had joined in too.

"Well," said Avishai. "I actually am interested in joining the chorus, but, well, I hate to sound stupid, but what would a voice lesson entail? We didn't have those at our old school."

"Hey, it's not a problem. Not all schools do voice lessons, but they are essentially a time, once a week, where we pull you out of class during a different class period each week. We work on your sound, the way that you fit in with the others' voices, what you need to improve, all of that good stuff. Then, later on in the year, we'll work on pieces that you have for auditions, sight reading, the works. If you're in the show in the spring, then we'll put you in a lesson group with people who you have scenes with. It's a lot of fun."

He nodded and smiled, they sounded like a lot of fun. "Really nice to meet you, Mr. Rattner," he said at last. He was excited but also a little intimidated by how seriously the school seemed to take their music. There were so many opportunities that he could have as a singer at this new school, it was impossible not to be both excited and overwhelmed at the same time.

"It was so nice to meet you all," Mr. Rattner called as Shelly was leading them down the hall. "Shelly, I'll see you tomorrow, Avishai, I hope to see you soon." Although this was all so new, Avishai was pretty sure Mr. Rattner would be seeing him soon enough.

"So," Shelly said to them once they were out of the chorus room and back into the purple hall. "Noah, you're the instrumentalist, right?"

"Yeah, I play the French horn."

Avishai was glad to have the attention off him for a moment.

"Would you like to see the band room, or is the French horn played in the orchestra? Sorry, I don't play anything and I'm kind of clueless when it comes to these sorts of things."

"No problem. It's kind of an obscure instrument, anyway. It's usually played in the band, because it's a brass instrument, but if the school has a symphonic orchestra or a full orchestra, which means that it has all instruments included, not just strings, then the French horn can play in that, too. Do you happen to know if that's the type of orchestra this school has?"

"Honestly, I don't know," she said, leading into one of the rooms. "The rooms look the same anyway, so I'll just show you the band one, but I'm sure you could talk to our instrumental program director. His name's Mr. Garlick, and he's super nice. I've never taken an instrument or anything, but he's my homeroom teacher and seriously the sweetest. I don't really know much else about the instrumental department, so are y'all ready to leave?"

When they nodded, led them out the door and back into the hallway. When they stepped through the door on the opposite side of the hall, it was into a brightly lit gymnasium.

"So," Shelly began. "Does anyone want to guess what this room might be?" They all laughed for a moment. "Anyway, this is the gym. We have different options for gym classes for every grade but the ninth graders. For tenth, eleventh, and twelfth grades, we offer team sports, Zumba, adventure games, things like that. Any idea what you'd want to do?"

Avishai considered the options. At their old school, they hadn't been given choices about their gym classes. They'd just played normal gym games like dodgeball, kickball, and they'd also had specific basketball, soccer, baseball, and football units. He had no idea what the girls did for their gym classes.

"Are the classes coed?" he asked. The Academy had always had separate gym classes for girls and boys, and neither group really talked about it. Actually, most of their classes were separate. Boys and girls took secular classes together as well as band, but chorus and all religious classes other than Hebrew were separate. The girls learned family law while the boys learned Talmud, the Gomorrah, and other things like that.

Shelly frowned. "Um, do you mean to ask if we allow both boys and girls and everyone else in our gym classes?" Avishai nodded. "Yeah, all of our classes are together. We have coed gym. I don't know what your old school had, but I'm sure that it's not all that much different."

Avishai was sure it would be, but he dropped the subject for now. He didn't feel like explaining Jewish modesty laws to Shelly. Another thought occurred to him, but this one was more just of a logistics question.

"Do we have to wear gym uniforms?"

She shook her head and laughed a little bit.

"We are a private school, yes. However, unlike most private schools, we don't have a uniform, or even a gym uniform. We do require that everyone change into gym clothes, though. You only need a T-shirt different from the one you wear to classes, and shorts or sweatpants or something. Oh, and sneakers. You can't participate unless you have socks and sneakers."

She checked her watch. "Well, I think it's time to go. I've held you guys captive for all of sixth period. Does anyone have any questions while we're walking out?" She took them back to the main doors and nudged one open for them, looking apologetic. "I don't mean to rush you, but I want to make sure you can get out of here before all the students trample you in their hurry to get out of here once the bell rings."

They all laughed and filed outside. Shelly gave them one last wave. "It was so nice to meet all of you. Avishai, Noah, I'll see you guys soon!"

CHAPTER THIRTEEN

So now Avishai and Noah had a school. They had created their schedules and made sure all of their documents from the Academy were on track to transfer properly. Although the Academy's administration didn't like them much, the secretary was still very helpful. When they were finished, they went home. An excited buzz floated in the car as they rode back with the radio turned to a classic rock station.

Avishai noticed something unusual: people. Throngs of them standing around, most with their cell phones out, leaning toward one another to whisper with wide eyes. Avishai recognized almost all of them as his neighbors, though he didn't know any of them that well.

What were they all so fascinated by?

And then he saw it.

His dad swore.

Written on their garage door were just two little words graffitied in black spray paint. Two words that cut deep into Avishai as though they had been carved into his skin by knives. He couldn't believe what he was seeing, but as the car crept closer to the house, there was no mistaking what had been scrawled on the garage door:

DIE FAGS.

All capital letters, as if he didn't know this person was yelling.

He could barely breathe, let alone say anything. Tears welled in his eyes, and he did nothing to keep them from spilling down his cheeks, unable to move. He just sat in the car, knowing that Noah and his dad were dealing with this too.

His dad was the first to move. "Hey!" he shouted, climbing out of the car. "Get out of here! This is none of your business. Move along."

People scattered from their property. Through his stunned haze, Avishai had to admit that whatever else could be said about his dad, he did know how to handle a crowd.

They pulled up to their property and into the driveway, but did not go into the garage. Instead, Avishai watched as his dad got out of the car. "You stay here," he said to Noah and Avishai. Both of them stayed in their seats while he walked to the garage door to inspect the damages.

Avishai was frozen to his seat. The elation from being accepted at Rainbow was long gone, and all he could feel now was… It wasn't only humiliation. It was fear, hatred, and humiliation, rolled together with the knowledge that this was because of him. Because of what he had done, what he had said. A crime had been committed because of him.

And not just any crime. A hate crime.

Avishai stayed with Noah while his dad assessed the damage, swearing all the while. Finally he returned to pull the car into the garage. Avishai got out shakily and followed his father and Noah into the house, his body on automatic. They stopped in the kitchen, but he didn't. He couldn't.

The house felt wrong now. Violated. By the time he got to his room, he couldn't steady his hands enough to twist his door lock. He slid down with his back to the door, tears streaming down his face.

He'd done this. He'd done this. If he wasn't a faggot, none of this would have happened...

~~*

Avishai sat in his room, shaking and crying. He was frustrated with himself for bringing this upon all of them. His dad and Noah could deny it, but he knew this was all his fault. If he hadn't been a faggot none of this would have happened. He hated that word but if *they* were going to use it then damn it he would too. All he had the power to do was rock back and forth on the bed, shaking his head and crying. He couldn't do anything to make this all go away.

Then he remembered the bottle of sleeping pills in the cabinet in the bathroom. The thought sobered him up, and his frustration and directionlessness were replaced suddenly by a cold certainty. *Am I really going to do this?* There had been so many times he had thought about, even fantasized about this. It was almost like it was a prophecy that he could do nothing about but put off. It had always been inevitable.

And now was the time.

He wiped the tears from his eyes carefully and breathed deeply to calm himself down. He didn't want anyone to think this was a rash decision. He thought about Noah and his dad, somewhere else in the house, probably mad as hell at him. He couldn't blame them. He was mad as hell at himself, too. He wanted to punish himself for all the stupid things he had done—for kissing Noah back in ninth grade, for continuing their relationship even though he knew nothing good could come out of it, for keeping that stupid notebook, for not denying this whole thing from the start. This would never have happened if he had just been straight, or at least pretended to be.

He stood, almost falling down with how wobbly his knees were. This just angered him more. God, how useless could he be? *It's time to man up,* he told himself. It was time to do this. He had to. He walked slowly to the bathroom, dragging his feet—or were his feet dragging him? He prayed to God that he wouldn't see anyone on his way there. If he saw his dad, or God forbid Noah, he knew that he wouldn't be able to go through with this. And he had to. He couldn't explain it, but he just knew he had to do this.

Step by step, he made his way to the bathroom, his hands clenched in both anger and fear. He felt a tear drip down from his eye but ignored it. Once in the bathroom, he shut the door and flicked on the lights, hoping he wouldn't make a sound. He didn't want anyone to disturb him. He looked through the bottles of pills until he found the sleeping pills. His dad had bought them for him when he said he was having trouble getting to sleep at night, but he had never taken them. He'd always wanted to be sure there would be enough for a lethal dose, he hoped. He didn't know how many he had to take for it to kill him, but he assumed a bottle full would be enough.

He double-checked to make sure that the door was locked before he opened the bottle. He stared down at the little red pills. They were so small, so harmless-looking. He wasn't sure how many to take, and cursed himself silently for forgetting his phone in his bedroom. He should have looked it up. He knew that if he went back to his room now he wouldn't be able to make it back. He would chicken out like everyone expected him to. No, he had to do this.

He counted out five pills, then ten. He wasn't sure if it would be enough, and he didn't want to screw this up, so he shook the rest of the contents into his hand and placed them on the counter before him. He filled up the mug by the sink with water—the same mug he had used since he was a kid to brush his teeth with at night. He gathered a few of the pills into his hand, took them, and drank a sip of water. He did this again and again until all the pills were gone, and only then did he notice the tears running down his cheeks. Frustrated, he wiped them away before taking one last look in the mirror. God, he looked like a mess. His shirt was wrinkled, his face was red, and his nose was running. He splashed some water on his face and reminded himself that it wouldn't matter in a few minutes.

He opened the door, walked back to his room—it seemed to be a shorter distance than when he had walked to the bathroom only a few minutes before—and laid down in his bed, staring up at the glow-in-the-dark stars on the ceiling. Tears blurred his eyes as he wondered if he would see his mom again, or if nothing would happen, if the world would just fade into black and then he would no longer be a part of it. Each of these thoughts both comforted and agitated him.

He pulled out his phone and plugged in his earbuds. He selected the song Stairway to Heaven, cliché though it was, because it had always soothed him and he wanted to be at peace in his last moments. Toward the end of the song, his eyelids started to get heavy. He felt himself falling asleep and didn't fight it. He heard the song end but was too tired to play it again. He laid in the dark, listening to nothing, and slowly felt himself fade away.

He couldn't remember everything, but there were flashes, like being shaken by Noah but unable to open his eyes or make a sound. *Just leave me alone* was his last thought before he was unconscious again. Then he was in an ambulance, with people all around him shouting and attaching him to machines. He prayed that they were too late, and felt himself slip into unconsciousness once more. It was in and out like this, for how long, he didn't know. He just hoped it would all be over soon.

But soon came and then he was awake. Alive. Surrounded by doctors and nurses he was groggily aware had made every effort to save him. He was humiliated beyond belief that he had failed and that all these people had worked so hard to save a life he didn't even want. He cried and cried while they asked him question after question. He decided it was no use to lie anymore, so he let everything come pouring out.

"I just don't deserve to be here anymore," he said quietly and through tears when a psychiatrist, a Dr. Gronblom, had asked him what made him feel like suicide was his only option. "No one needs me or wants me. I only cause my dad pain. He's embarrassed to have a gay son and he never liked me to begin with. I just wish I had never existed."

He was handed a tissue, which he soaked

through in a minute. Dr. Gronblom just sat there and let him talk. Avishai told him everything, about how his mom had died and his father had been distant. How he had been so happy with Noah when things were still a secret, but that now everything was ruined. Especially now.

Dr. Gronblom nodded and took notes, asking a few questions but mostly letting Avishai speak. He told him that the doctors had put a sedative into his IV, and Avishai was thankful for it. It seemed like for the first time his brain was going slow enough that he could understand it. He felt calm, like he had right before he'd gone unconscious.

"I don't like feeling like that," he told Dr. Gronblom after a moment's silence. "I don't like feeling out of control and like I can't stop myself. It's an exhausting feeling, like I'm just stalling until I kill myself."

"You shouldn't have to feel like that," the doctor told Avishai. "No one should. We need to find a treatment for your depression that actually works for you. It'll be hard, but we'll find something so this doesn't happen again. And I'm going to set you up with an excellent therapist who specializes in gay teens. You're going to have to put in effort to work with them to make you well again, but are you willing to do that?"

Avishai nodded, truly believing for the first time that he could feel better one day.

"Good, because you are an exceptional young

person and you deserve to make it through this." He tugged a notepad out of his pocket. "Right now, what I'm going to do is write you a prescription for an antidepressant. Now, this one might not be the one that works best for you, and it won't make you feel better immediately, but I want you to bear with it and take it as prescribed, and if you do that and start going to therapy, I really think you can get better. Do you think you can do that?"

Avishai nodded again, somewhat relieved that this man wasn't lecturing him, but instead trying to help.

The door opened and a nurse came in, smiling. He bent to whisper something in Dr. Gronblom's ear.

"Your family is here," the doctor said as the nurse slipped out.

Avishai instantly felt himself grow anxious. They had to be so disappointed in him.

The doctor looked from the heart monitor and then back to Avishai, and must have understood. "Do you want me to tell them you're resting?" he asked kindly.

Avishai shook his head. He needed to face them. He needed to apologize for what he had put them through. If he was going to get better, it needed to start with them.

"Okay," the doctor said, patting his hand—the one without the IV in it—and leaving the room. A moment later, his dad and Noah shuffled in, slowly and unsurely. They both had red-rimmed eyes, and he immediately felt guilty. Seeing that made him want to cry, but he knew he had to stay strong for them. He needed to show that he was going to fight to get better.

Noah walked right to the bed before falling to his knees and breaking down in tears. Avishai edged his hand to the side of the bed, and rubbed his back, whispering, "Shh, shh," to him. This made Noah cry even harder.

Avishai looked up and watched as his father—always so stoic and unfeeling—clenched and unclenched his fists and his jaw and brought his right hand up to his mouth each time he appeared to be starting to cry.

Avishai knew he had to speak.

"I'm—I'm so sorry," he said.

The anger on his father's face melted away as he approached the bed, smoothed the hair on Avishai's sweaty forehead, and whispered, "I'm just glad that you're alive."

"Noah," Avishai said, his voice hoarse and nearly choked out by his large tears. "I'm so sorry. I—I—normally I can control this, I can keep it inside, I can be okay. And I have never tried to hurt myself before, you have to believe me." He tried to continue but was immediately overcome by tears.

Only then was Noah finally able to find his voice. "Hey, hey," he soothed. "It's okay. I mean, it's not, but you're alive, and right now you are going to be just fine. Ooshy, I love you, and I will always be here for you. You need, need, *need* to remember that. I will always be here for you, whenever you feel like this, whenever you need me. But you have to be here for me too, and I'm pretty sure that if you're six feet under then you can't exactly help me all that much." Maybe it was inappropriate to laugh, but they did anyway, overcome by so many emotions.

"Avishai, I thought about it too, you know," his dad said suddenly, cutting off the laughter. "I thought about killing myself. It was right after your mom died. It was just so hard for me. I mean, I know how hard it was on you, too. You were just a kid. You still are, for God's sake, but it was just so hard to lose her. It wasn't the fact that she was—that she was dead. I think that it was more just that she wasn't there for us anymore.

"Realizing that when I came home, she wasn't there. The knowledge that she and I would never be able to—to have the chance to grow old together, like we had always planned. Knowing that she would never see you graduate, or get a job, become an adult, make something of the life, your life, that she and I created together. Knowing that when your grades started to go down, it was my fault, because I wasn't there to help you like she always had. It was just so much to bear."

Avishai felt uncomfortable. His dad had always been so strong and capable, and now to find out it wasn't so simple? He wondered what would have happened to him if his dad *had* died. He couldn't even imagine losing both parents.

His father continued before he was able to find his words. "For the first year, I didn't know how I was going to manage. How *we* were going to manage. I didn't know if I was strong enough to be a single parent and to raise you on my own and still be able to be a congressman. It was a very, very dark time for me, one that I thought was gone from me, but it sneaks back every now and again. I was selfish, and I wasn't thinking of you. I was carrying around a great sadness inside of me, and—and I almost lost control. I thought about killing myself. I thought about it more than I should have, really. I did a lot of drinking and I thought, Why the hell not? I'm already miserable as all hell, why is it worth it? Why is life worth living?

"And you were there. My son, and I almost left you here, all alone, because I was selfish, and because I wasn't thinking. I couldn't see past the dark times we were in. I couldn't imagine a place or a time where life could or would ever be any better. I was stuck where I was. I was stuck in a puddle of depression and alcohol and loneliness. And you, Avishai, you are the reason that I never acted on all of those thoughts. Avishai, I wanted to, believe me, but I didn't. I didn't because I didn't want you to have to be an orphan. Because I didn't want you to have to go through foster care and feel miserable and unloved. I knew that, for your sake, I would have to pull it together. And so I did.

"I saw you, so young and impressionable, and I knew that I needed to change, if for your sake only, but also for mine. I needed you to be there as my lifeline. You pulled me back from my despair. You were the reason that I made the change. I stopped drinking as much, I started to see a therapist, and made sure that I never felt that way again. I don't care what you need, son. Whatever help you need, you will get it. I will help, and Noah can help..."

Avishai looked over to Noah, who wiped the tears from his face before taking Avishai's hand in his own. "I'm here for you, baby." Avishai couldn't hold his gaze for fear he would fall apart again. "I will always be here for you, no matter what you need. I will always remind you why you're here, and why you need to be here, right by my side, always, no matter how bad things get. Ooshy, your dad and I, we love you so, so much. It hurts us to see you like this, and I promise you that things can and will turn around for you. You just have to let them."

"Avishai," his dad chimed in, "Noah and I, and whomever else you want around in your life, we will always do what is right by you. We will take care of you, we will get you the help that you need, whatever that may happen to include. We, or rather you, I suppose, are going to have to start going to see a therapistagain. Or if not him, then at least someone. Your doctor recommended someone else—you can decide. I know it's hard, but you need to try, for me. I can't, can't, *can't* lose you, Avishai. I simply refuse to. You need to get better, I guess is all I'm trying to say. I know what this is like. I know exactly how hard this must be for you, because believe me, I have felt exactly the same. I have wanted to do what you tried to do today, and I came back from it. I faced it, and now it is your turn. You have to."

He turned abruptly and walked to the farthest corner of the room, holding his hands behind his back, and sniffed deeply.

"So," he said after a long pause. "You will be kept here for observation as well as just to make sure that you didn't kill your liver or your kidneys entirely. Also, they need to keep you here for a seventy-two-hour watch. At that point they will administer a psychiatric exam to determine whether or not you are fully able to be out of the hospital and to not be in any way harmful to yourself or to others." He walked back toward the bed and smiled a little.

"I know, Dad," he whispered tiredly. The sedatives were starting to make him feel fuzzy and tired. "The doctor already told me all that."

"Okay, well, forgive me," his dad said, smiling. "I just want to make sure you know what's going on. Anyway, if they find they you are in fact all right in the head," and he rapped his knuckles gently on Avishai's head. "Then they will let you come home with me." He looked back at Noah.

"Us. You can come home with us."

Avishai was grateful, but didn't release his grasp on Noah's hand. "I'm okay, really. I mean— well, I think I'm all right. I don't even know why I did this. I just, it's just...I don't know. I don't even know why I did this. I have you, Noni," he said, looking up at his boyfriend. "And Dad, I've got you, and you still love me. And I've got a great new school to go to, I just, oh God, I don't even know. I feel like I owe you guys some sort of explanation. But I can't tell you why I did this, because I honestly don't know why. I didn't get kicked out of the house like you, Noah." He looked up at Noah, who should have been the one in this situation of either of them. "I just— sometimes I feel so sad. That sounds like a really stupid reason to try to kill myself, just being sad. I just can't always keep it in. Sometimes, like that time a few weeks ago, Dad, when you asked me to move up to DC with you."

His dad looked purely aghast. "Avishai, I'm so, so sorry. I had no idea that...I was just trying to be nice. I missed you so much. I always do. Every day of the week that I'm not here, when I'm in DC, I miss you. Unbelievably so. You're my only family. I was just trying to give you an opportunity to not be alone five days of the week."

"Dad, Dad, Dad. The point is, I wasn't so upset because you asked me to move, it was just that I would have to leave Noah here. I didn't want to leave without him. I was just so stressed. And now, with all that's happening, with Noah getting kicked out of his house and moving in with us, with the old school, and now with the Rainbow Alliance Alternative School... And then that stupid graffiti. You got out of the car, and you looked so, so pissed, Dad. You looked embarrassed by us, that this had happened. And, well, I don't know. The way that l saw it, if I wasn't gay, if none of this was going on, then, then you would have been so much happier. If I hadn't done that stupid press conference, if you had never found out, if Noah and I had never dated, if we had just ignored this, then, then, well, literally none of this would have ever happened."

"Avishai," his dad interrupted, putting a hand up. "No. Just stop talking, son. You're wrong. You are dead wrong. All of this would have happened. I know that maybe we wouldn't have had to face it this soon if it wasn't for Noah here. Not that I blame you either, kiddo. But right now, no matter what you two guys would have done, you would still be gay. It wouldn't matter if the two of you were together or not. The only difference would be that maybe you boys wouldn't have come out, but you would be so miserable and so, so alone.

"But who's to say that neither of the two of you would have fallen in love with someone else and come out, or just come out anyway. Or be outed by some idiot homophobe who was trying to hurt one of you, or your families. The thing is, I could care less about the..."

Avishai cut him off. "Dad," he said, laughing. "I think you mean 'I *couldn't* care less.' Sorry, continue."

Noah chuckled a little and smiled. Avishai caught the smile and returned it.

"Sorry, Mr. Miller," Noah said once he had stopped his giggling. "That drives me crazy, when people say 'could care less.' I've been correcting Avishai for years. I guess I'm finally starting to rub off on him." Avishai and Noah laughed a little more, but his dad didn't seem to get what was so funny. It all seemed utterly absurd, to be laughing about something as stupid as grammar, but it did release some of the tension.

His dad shook his head at them. "I'm sorry, what was I saying again?"

"I think that you were saying something about how you could and at the same could not care less about," Avishai told him, still teasing.

"You two are a couple of no good smartasses, aren't you?" He smiled slightly. "But thank you, son. Anyway, yeah. I could *not* care less what some asshole, pardon my French, wrote on our garage door. It doesn't matter. It's paint. It's going to take ten minutes with a paintbrush to get rid of their beautiful handiwork. But it doesn't even matter. I don't care. I'm not mad at you. How the hell could I be mad at you? You're my kid and I love you. Period. What other people think, it doesn't matter. I don't care about their opinions. Don't you ever, either one of you, feel like that isn't true.

"I have, in the past week, gotten maybe one to two hundred emails about you. Other than a handful of stupid homophobes who don't matter sending me and my office their babbling nonsensical shit, they've all been saying that you two are admirable and inspirational. Parents have told me that they are able to better deal with their gay, lesbian, bisexual and or trans kids because they have our family as a role model. I was going to tell you two guys later, but this whole story broke right in the middle of a slow news cycle and people are finding this fascinating, so we've been offered news and radio interviews.

"I mean, I'm not sitting here and talking to you two about The Atlanta Chronicles or some other such waste of paper faux news source like that. No, I mean that we are getting offers from *The New York Times*, *People Magazine*, The Ellen Show, the Today Show. Oprah freaking Winfrey said that she would fly us down to do an interview live on her show, but she also said she finds you truly inspirational and can't wait to meet you. The both of you," he exclaimed, looking at both Noah and Avishai, now.

"Just about everyone who is looking for an interview is asking for you, too, Noah."

Noah looked slightly surprised. "Why would anyone want to talk to me?" he asked. "After all, you guys are really the interesting ones. I just came along for the ride."

Avishai shook his head. "Noni, you are so much more than that. I love you so much, even if you aren't as well-known by the small percentage of Americans who are at all well-informed news-wise." He laughed a little.

"But really," Avishai's dad said to them. "In all seriousness, Noah, you are America's gay sweetheart. Avishai is too, breaking down a mountain of political barriers by himself and through me. And you," he said, turning in Noah's direction to look and point at him. "If what everyone has been telling about the political barriers, then what you have broken can be described in no other way than a freaking shitload of social stereotypes."

Noah blushed a little.

"No, really, kid," he implored. "No joke. You've broken all the stereotypes. That's not to say that Avishai fit the picture one hundred and ten percent, but you, Noah...you are six-foot-one, muscular as all hell. If someone would ever dare to call you a faggot, well then, I just don't even know what would happen. Look, point is, kid, you aren't the traditional picture of a queer." He flinched. "Sorry, that's really offensive, isn't it?"

Noah and Avishai looked at one another before responding to Avishai's dad on what was probably going to be a very lengthy and drawn out process, when it came down right to it. They had actually, Noah and Avishai, begun the very arduous and lengthy process of creating a tactic with which to approach him on this. They had only come up with one thing so far: be very cautious when dealing with quasi-homophobic conservative Jewish congressmen.

"Well," he began cautiously. "Think about it this way. How would you feel if someone called you queer?"

"Probably I would feel like beating the ever-living shit out of the guy."

Avishai groaned and glared at his father, but just then Noah started laughing. Avishai shot Noah an ice-cold glance, but he couldn't really be mad. He knew Noah would beat anyone up for him if it ever came to that.

"Not exactly my point.," he said. "But I like the enthusiasm and I can't exactly argue with your intended response, although I would suggest that either one of you, if the situation may arise, give the poor bastard a good twenty-second running head start before the chase begins. I would guess that you would not really like getting called that, am I right?"

"Ha, I guess that you could say that again." His dad laughed bitterly.

"And so I would guess that any other harsher term, like for example, faggot, or fairy, or something, that you would probably react in around the same or in a harsher manner." Avishai looked at his dad, who in turn looked back at him and nodded in a way that made Avishai think his dad might be getting it. "It's the exact same way when someone calls a gay person a nasty name like that. It doesn't matter that it actually applies to them. If someone called you a kike, then you would probably, to use your words, 'beat the ever-living shit' out of that person, am I right?"

When his dad nodded solemnly, he took it as a hint that he had gotten the message, but felt a need to thoroughly drive their point home. "It's the exact same way. So, if you call anyone, no matter who they are, a name that you would feel in any way offended or insulted being called, then my expert advice to you would be to think twice before calling them that."

"Oh, ha, yeah, I think I get it now."

"Oh," Noah continued after getting such a positive response. "Also, you probably shouldn't say that something is gay, either." Avishai looked up at his dad, who was now looking just a little bit confused and also somewhat irritated. *Damn it,* he thought. *We pushed too hard.* But, to his surprise, his dad seemed less angry and more concerned when he continued.

"But why does it even matter? I mean, it isn't an insult, it's just a colloquialism. It's just an expression. It doesn't mean anything, really, and it's not exactly like I'm trying to be insulting. It's just like saying that something is retarded. I'm not saying that it actually is, so, it doesn't have the same connotations, right?" his dad asked confidently, as if he had made a fairly convincing argument.

"Um, actually no," Noah said. "What does it mean when you say that something is gay, Mr. Miller? Or even for that matter, when you refer to something as retarded?"

His dad stayed silent, probably assuming that this was a rhetorical question and that the answers would be soon provided. Avishai hoped Noah was going to let him sweat it out a little, and to his delight, Noah did.

"Well, I've never really thought about it, I guess," his dad admitted.

"Most people," Noah said, "when they use a term like that, use it with connotations that would tend to taint the meaning of a word or phrase from its original face value. You're saying that something is gay, or retarded, but really what you are trying to say is that whatever you happen to be referring to is stupid, right?"

Avishai breathed a sigh of relief as his father nodded and listened. He watched as his dad blushed deeper and deeper with each of the carefully selected words that Noah said.

"So, really, you are using whatever term that you have chosen, which I am assuming does not apply to this, well, whatever it is that you are inappropriately describing at the moment, as a synonym for stupid, am I right?"

I get what you mean, kid," his dad said after a moment "You're saying that by the way that I'm using the word or the phrase, the 'connotations,' as you said, I'm making it into something that is disrespectful, right?"

Avishai grinned. His dad had actually gotten it. "Yes, exactly."

"Ok, I really think that I understand," his dad replied after another moment or so of silent thought. "And what is more than that, kid, is that I liked the way you said it. You clearly stated your opinion in a manner that made me see your side of the argument without wanting to kick your ass. In other words, it was very diplomatic, the way you voiced your opinion just now."

"Um thanks?" Noah said, looking confused. He turned to look at Avishai, who shrugged, and they both in turn looked back at Avishai's dad.

"Noah, this may seem a little strange," Avishai's dad began warily, "but have you put any thought at all into what you might want to be when you grow up?"

Oh God, Avishai thought to himself. He was trying to recruit Noah for something.

"With all due respect, Mr. Miller..." Noah began. Avishai chuckled. He knew that that was never a very good way to start a reply. "Um, well, Avishai and I are juniors. This year is pretty much devoted to finding out which career path to take and where it will lead. And where you want it to lead you. Well, what I'm saying is, yes. What I've thought is that I would like to be a lawyer. Maybe civil work, maybe defense litigation. Either that or having something to do with international affairs. I'm still figuring out the specifics... Either way, law school, if I can get in and if I can afford it, will most definitely be in my post-college future."

Avishai's dad looked satisfied with that answer. Slyly, he asked, "Noah, have you given any thought at all to maybe going into politics?" Avishai watched the look on Noah's face shift from surprised to bashful as he thought for a moment before carefully choosing just the right words with care and then finally responding.

Before he could speak, Avishai did. "Psst, Noah. It's a trap!" he shouted, cupping his fingers and holding them to the side of his head in the best fashion that he could manage in an attempt to resemble Admiral Ackbar.

Noah laughed out loud at Avishai's crummy impersonation of the creature's huge eyes. Despite Avishai and his warning, Noah proceeded anyway, saying, "I'd be lying to you if I said that I've never considered it. The only reason I thought about it at all is because I watched *The West Wing*. When I first started to watch it, I saw myself really wanting to become a politician, or maybe do something behind the scenes, like be a campaign organizer or publicist or campaign consultant or something."

His dad looked over at Noah and smiled. "Atta boy."

"I don't know." Noah chuckled to himself. "It just seemed so glamorous and appealing at the time. So, I started to think about how to go about becoming a politician. Based off of the Internet and the information that I have found regarding the subject, it would appear as though the majority of politicians first start off their careers as lawyers.

"So that got me thinking about becoming a lawyer, and what sort of law I would want to practice. I thought for a while on this, and the more I thought about it, the more I realized that I really wanted to be a lawyer, and not just as a stepping stone to a career in politics. As a defense attorney or doing civil cases, especially, I was thinking that maybe I could do some things with discrimination, I could really do a lot of good."

"Hey, sorry to interrupt," Avishai said. They both turned to him, as if they had, to some extent, forgotten where they were and that he was there with them too. "But it's pretty late, and you guys should probably get going. Don't get me wrong, I love hearing the two of you go back and forth, but it's getting so late, and I really just need to sleep right now. You guys probably do too."

"We can stay…" Noah started.

Avishai cut him off. "Really. You guys should be heading home."

His dad glanced at his watch. "Holy shit! It's only a few minutes to midnight!"

Noah looked incredulously at the clock that hung above the entrance to the hospital room. Sure enough, there were only a few short minutes until Friday morning began.

At some point during the duration of their

visit with Avishai, the two had gravitated to the two chairs in his room. But now they gathered their things, obviously tired now that they knew how late it was.

"Hey, kiddo," his dad said to him once he was stationed off to the bed's left side. "We don't have to go. We can stay here, for as long as you need us to. We just want to make sure that you are okay for us to leave before we do." He said this last part while brushing a few stray strands of hair out of Avishai's tired eyes.

"Really, Dad, I'm all right for you guys to leave," he said, moving his hair back in place. "There are about a million doctors here, at least two million nurses, and I've got my own personal psychiatrist. Really, I don't think that it would be possible for me to do anything without maybe one hundred or so people noticing. Trust me," he said. "I will not kill myself if you guys leave."

"Well, okay, if you insist. But there is a phone right there," he said, pointing at the phone by Avishai's bedside, "and you can call me whenever you want to or need to. Whatever time it is. Avishai, I'm your father, and I love you and care about you just so much more than you could ever understand. All right?"

"All right," Avishai echoed. "But really, Dad, I understand that I shouldn't have done this. Believe me, I'm not an idiot. I promise you I'm going to work so hard with the therapist and always take my meds. I want to get better."

His dad nodded and then leaned down to give him a tight hug. "I love you, kid."

"I know. I love you too, Dad."

Noah stayed behind as Avishai's dad left the room.

"Ooshy," he said, tears already forming in the corners of his eyes. "The second you start to feel like this again, if ever you do, come and find me. I don't care what is happening, you can never hurt yourself. Ever. It sounds so corny, but things really will get better. I promise. I will always be here for you. I can't let you ever do this again. I don't think that I could ever live without you. You have to believe me that things will end up right by you. By us. We will end up together, and everything will work out. I love you, Ooshy. Never, ever forget. I won't let you."

Avishai was trying so hard to hold back the tears the best that he could. He held on tightly to Noah's hand and pulled him down to his level, then, mindful of his IV, wrapped his arms around him and closed his eyes tightly. "I love you so, so much. You have to believe me that the last thing that I would ever want is to hurt you, especially like this. I was just so selfish and I wasn't thinking at all about you. I'm so, so sorry, baby."

By now there was no point in either of them even attempting to block the fresh cascade of new tears that came rushing from each of them. "It's all right," Noah said. "I love you so much. Don't you ever dare forget it."

"I wouldn't dream of it. I love you too, Noni."

Noah pulled himself up and gave Avishai a kiss.

His dad cleared his throat from the doorway.

Avishai and Noah sprang apart. Or really, Noah sprang off Avishai. Both of them blushed deeply. Noah walked wordlessly to where Avishai's dad was waiting for him.

"Avishai, we'll be back tomorrow. I'll see you later, son."

Noah waved gently with just his fingers as he and Avishai's dad exited the room. Avishai waved back with just the faintest hint of a smile. And so, with the promise to see each other the following day, they went their separate ways. Just after Avishai saw his dad and Noah leave the room, he gave in to his exhaustion and fell asleep.

EPILOGUE

The next two days flew by in a blur, with both Noah and Avishai's dad visiting him in the hospital. At times he just slept, but the nurses told him later that Noah and his dad simply sat there in his room while he did. At other times, when Avishai was awake, they would sit and talk to him, not really saying much, just speaking about what was going on in the rest of the world. Although Avishai had insisted that they go to *shul* on Saturday morning without him, for Shabbat services, they decided in the end to stay with him, not because they didn't trust his judgement in their absence, but just because they didn't want him to have to be alone for so long.

Then, late on Sunday night, the psychiatrist he had met with on the night he had been admitted—which seemed to have been so long ago—gave him an evaluation. Noah and his dad were asked to leave the room. They did so, and within the hour, Avishai was cleared for discharge. They went home that night and said little on the ride there and even less when they arrived back home.

It was an uncertain sensation for Avishai to return home after the whole ordeal, even though both Noah and his dad had assured him that they had repainted the garage door. He was stressed, but wasn't quite sure why. He was better than he had been, but still felt uneasy and couldn't pay much attention to whatever TV show his dad had turned on to fill the silence. As the time approached to retire to his room, he began to dread his re-entrance more and more.

As they were getting ready for bed that night, Avishai went to the guest room to talk to Noah.

"I don't know if I can do this," he said. Noah looked confused, so Avishai explained, "I don't know if I can go back in there, into my room. I know how dumb that sounds, but I feel like it's returning to the scene of the crime or something. Does it even count as a crime if it's self-inflicted? God, it doesn't matter. That's not the point. The point is, I feel like I can't go in there."

"Babe," Noah began tiredly, rubbing his eyes, which were red from crying so much that weekend. "It's just a room. Something happened in that room that wasn't supposed to and so some feelings are associated with that. I understand that, you have to believe me. But you are not the same person who you were on Thursday night. Or rather, that was not who you, who Avishai Benjamin Miller, is. That was a person who was afraid of the world. That was a person who was done with dealing, and that was a person who had simply given up. That person is not the same as the person who stands here before me right now.

"The person who I see standing in front of me

right now is the real you. He is unafraid and unapologetic. He knows that he has people to go to when things get rough, people like his loving boyfriend and his father. He knows that suicide is never the answer, and he knows that tomorrow, when we go to Rainbow, things will start to get better. He knows that he can't give up, and that's the guy that I fell in love with."

Noah looked into Avishai's eyes with such devotion and love that it made him ache. If he had succeeded in killing himself, then poor, sweet Noah would have been left totally alone in this world. Avishai wrapped his arms around his boyfriend and gave him a giant squeeze.

"Thank you," Avishai whispered into Noah's ear while they embraced. "Thank you so, so much. For everything. I think that I needed to hear that. I love you, Noni. Let's go to bed, big day tomorrow."

"I love you too, Ooshy," Noah replied, still hugging him. After a moment they separated, and Avishai went into his room.

He sat on his bed for what seemed like forever. He kept envisioning what he had done just a few nights before. Tears sprang yet again to his eyes, but he tried to blink them away. He had promised his dad and Noah that he would try to get better, so he took a deep breath and let it go slowly. He repeated this for several moments until he was calm enough to lie down and fall asleep, worrying about the next day at school.

He didn't sleep well, tossing and turning time and time again as the moments ticked by until his new life was going to begin. Still, his eyes sprang open when he heard his alarm, suddenly awake and energized-ready for the day.

He wiped his eyes, which felt crusty from tears, and went to the bathroom to wash his face with cold water to wake himself up and calm himself down. He brushed his teeth and hair, reminding himself over and over that starting today things would get better. When he went downstairs, dressed in the same button down and slacks outfit he would have worn to the RHA, he was greeted by a smiling Noah.

"Good morning, love," Noah said as he got out the fixings for breakfast—bowls, spoons, cereal, and milk.

"Good morning, Noni," Avishai replied cheerfully, kissing Noah lightly on the cheek. He felt an extra bit of pep in place of his usual nervousness. He just had a feeling that things were going to go well today. They were going to have their first day at their new school, and then he had an appointment with Dr. Schwartz, the therapist the psychiatrist from the hospital had recommended.

"Is your dad always gone this early?" Noah asked.

"Usually. On Mondays he wakes up at around five o'clock and is at the airport in a half hour. It doesn't take all that long to fly to DC, so he usually leaves early on Monday morning instead of late on Sunday night like most of the other congressmen have to do."

"Oh," Noah replied. "That's nice, I guess. I mean, you get to spend a bit of extra time with him, right?"

"Yeah, I guess," he said after a moment. Thinking about it, though, it didn't really matter, as those few hours were spent asleep anyway. If he didn't see his father for almost five days straight, did it really matter all that much where he spent one night? Avishai didn't think so, but still, his father had chosen to spend the previous night here instead of in his apartment in Washington, so maybe there were a few extra hours spent with one another, even if they had been spent sleeping. He had of course offered to stay as long as Avishai needed him to, but Avishai had insisted their routine get back to normal. Avishai and Noah ate their breakfasts silently. At seven, they got into Noah's car and began their fifty-three-minute drive to the Rainbow Alliance Alternative School. Classes didn't start until eight thirty, but Avishai wanted to leave the house with plenty of time to be sure they weren't tardy. What sort of first impression would that leave?

The drive there was nearly silent, except for the radio, which Noah kept fiddling with as he drove. He flicked incessantly through the stations on the radio, never settling on one for more than a moment.

Avishai tuned everything out and focused on his hands, which he was busy wringing. He held them so tightly his knuckles were white, but he barely noticed.

Of the two, he had always been the less social one. He was shy and often came off as snobby because if it. That was why he had always been so concerned with first impressions. They pulled into the parking lot at 8:05 and tried to go inside, only to find the front doors still locked. That gave them a few free minutes to sit in Noah's car before they had to face their new classmates

"Ooshy," Noah said. "You can't be nervous. I don't care if you are or not, just pretend like you aren't and you won't be. Fake it until you make it, do whatever it is that you have to, but you can't be nervous. This is a school that is completely a judgement-free zone. Go in there and be real. Be the full, real, unadulterated Avishai Miller, and I swear to you, you will love it and they will love you."

Avishai blushed deeply, his cheeks growing warm and pink. He had to blink to keep from crying yet again, but this time from happiness and love. God, he was so lucky to have Noah by his side. He smiled broadly and whispered, "I love you so much. Why did you choose me?"

Noah smiled sheepishly and stifled a little chuckle before he answered. "I saw through the shy you. I worked hard to find the real you, the one underneath. You keep it hidden away and you try to not let people see it. But you have to. If no place else, then show your real you here, at this new school. That is who I fell in love with, and that is who you are. And if you hate everyone here, then just think of me. And remember: love will always win out. We will get through this. We have gotten through everything else, it stands to reason that we can face high school."

And so, when other students began filtering into the parking lot and a staffer came to unlock the front doors, they walked into their new school. They walked hand-in-hand and prepared to face the new day in a new place with new people, but Avishai knew that together, they could get through it. Suddenly, the lyrics to *Eli Eli* fluttered through his head: *"Oh Lord, my God, I pray that these things never end."*

Fin

About the Author

Sarah is studying at Wellesley College (class of 2020) but is originally from the snowy city of Syracuse, New York. She wrote this book when she was 15 as part of National Novel Writing Month (NaNoWriMo.) When she isn't writing she can be found wherever there's a dog. Go ahead and like her page on facebook—Sarah L. Young Author—for more news and updates about her publications.

A Honeyed Light

FREDDIE MILANO

MAGNIFIED

MELL EIGHT

BARBARA GEIGER

Checking

INTO

Sodom

THE
LIFE
&
DEATH
OF
ELI *&* JAY

FRANCIS GIDEON

A.F. HENLEY
WE THREE
KINGS

95415178R00112

Made in the USA
San Bernardino, CA
16 November 2018